"Would you kiss me again?"

"What?" Cody's head reared back, and he looked at her in amazement. "Why the hell would you want me to do that?"

Tana scrambled through her mind for a reason other than that she just wanted to try it again. "Because I liked it. Didn't you?"

He just stared at her. Then, shaking his head in disbelief, he exploded with, "Are you really that naive? Look around you. You see anyone ready to rush to your rescue when things get out of hand?"

Tana frowned at him, baffled because he seemed angry. "Things won't get out of hand."

"How the hell do you know that?" he shouted. "You don't know the first thing about me! What happens if I decide a kiss isn't enough?"

MELINDA CROSS would love her readers to believe she was kidnapped as a child by an obscure nomadic tribe and rescued by a dashing adventurer. Actually, though, she is a wonderfully imaginative American writer who is married to a true romantic. Every spring, without fail, when the apple orchard blooms, her husband gathers a blanket, glasses and wine and leads Melinda out to enjoy the fragrant night air. Romantic fantasy? Nonsense, she says. This is the stuff of real life.

Books by Melinda Cross

HARLEQUIN PRESENTS
847—LION OF DARKNESS
889—A VERY PRIVATE LOVE
914—WHAT'S RIGHT
959—THE CALL OF HOME
1224—ONE HOUR OF MAGIC
1247—KING OF THE MOUNTAIN

MELINDA CROSS

a defiant dream

Harlequin Books

TORONTO • NEW YORK • LONDON
AMSTERDAM • PARIS • SYDNEY • HAMBURG
STOCKHOLM • ATHENS • TOKYO • MILAN

Harlequin Presents first edition November 1990
ISBN 0-373-11312-9

Original hardcover edition published in 1989
by Mills & Boon Limited

CHAPTER ONE

TANA MITCHELL stood quite still, light from the window she faced breaking around the slender, tense lines of her body. It was an ugly light for midmorning, tinged with the colour of crushed violets that always foretold bad weather. Storm, she thought. Tomorrow; Friday at the latest.

Her short, fine brows lowered over dark eyes that dominated the pale oval of her face as she focused on the distant peaks of the Big Snowy Mountain Range looming in the distance outside the window. As a child, she had thought of the mountains as sturdy sentinels on constant, benevolent watch over the place and the people she loved.

'They're the enemy, more often than not,' her father had told her, trying to dispel her childish fancies. 'They catch the rain and keep it from us in the months we need it most, then call the storms in winter to bury us under snow. There's nothing kind about those moutains, girl.'

And, of course, he had been right. So why had he stayed here? Why, when the mountains had taken so much, had he insisted on living in their shadow?

She stared coldly out of the window at Montana's unforgiving early winter landscape, dominated by the awesome peaks.

Damn them anyway, she thought bitterly. And

damn the whole state of Montana, while you're at it, and particularly this ranch. It had taken her mother, almost before she'd had a chance to know her; and now, years later, the mountains had claimed her father, too. You couldn't beat the mountains. You could fight them your whole life long, but you couldn't beat them.

She tossed her head impatiently, rearranging the long, black curls that fell to her shoulders and beyond. Her face looked vulnerable with the dark, curly mass as a frame, and her slender build enhanced the image; but there was a stubbornness in the eyes that gave the lie to the picture, a flash of black determination behind the liquid brown that belonged only here, with the snow-topped craggy spires as a background.

Her eyes swept over the hills that rolled up to the closest mountain, narrowing at every scraggly tree, at every outcropping, as if she actually expected that a cow would pop out of the shadows and end the deadly game of hide-and-seek before it began. And it had to begin soon. The colour of the sky told her that time was running out.

Somewhere in the high country, in the thousands of unfenced acres of federal grazing land, roamed a bull named Pillar and a hundred bred cows; the last of the great herd that had belonged to her father. It wasn't much of a herd—not in cattle country where stock was normally counted in the thousands—but Pillar's bloodlines were invaluable. If he'd bred with only half of the heifers turned loose with him last spring, the calves would sell for enough to save this ranch her father had loved so much. All she had to do was go up into the mountains, find them, and bring them back down to winter in the valley. All by herself. With a blizzard coming.

She pressed a strong, square hand to her forehead and closed her eyes. It was a crazy idea. Why was she even considering it? She didn't love the place any more. She'd run from it like a rabbit almost six years before, finding college and a teaching career in Chicago infinitely preferable to the constant struggle to survive that marked life in the mountainous wilderness of the American west. Let the contract holder repossess the Mitchell Ranch now that her father was gone. Let D.C. Enterprises, whoever the hell they were, take the place, and all the pain and heartache and death that went with it. She shouldn't care—and yet somewhere deep in her emotional make-up was one particularly stubborn Mitchell gene that bridled at the thought of giving up anything without a struggle, and that single gene was walking all over any vestige of good sense she might have had.

Tana turned away from the window and walked aimlessly around the large room that had been her father's office, brushing familiar objects with her fingertips as she passed, trying to find some comfort in the material things her father had cherished. She paused at the large oak desk that held a number of framed pictures and smiled wistfully into the pretty young face of a mother she could barely remember. The glass in the frame was so highly polished that she could see her own reflection superimposed over the likeness. The similarity of line and bone-structure startled her, as it always did.

She lifted her head towards the sound of the heavy front door opening then closing out in the entry hall, then smiled involuntarily at the tall, ruggedly handsome figure who appeared in the doorway a moment later. He looked almost the same today as he had when he'd signed on as foreman of Mitchell Ranch when Tana was only sixteen, nine years ago. He was a man of straight lines and sharp angles, with a lean, hard body and strong features that looked as if they had been chiselled out of unyielding rock. He spoke little and smiled even less, but his black eyes glittered with a pure, masculine intensity that still made her catch her breath whenever he looked at her.

'Tana.'

She closed her eyes briefly, cringing at the sound of her own name. How her parents must have loved this place, to name their only child after the state that would ultimately kill them both. She was constantly correcting everyone's mispronunciation. 'No, *Tana*, just like the state. Mon—*tana*.'

But even if the name seemed wrong, the deep, masculine voice that spoke it sounded right. It was the kind of voice that ought to echo through an oversized house like this.

'Hello, Zach.'

His mouth curved through the dark stubble of an unshaven chin in a pained smile. 'I wanted to say goodbye before I left for my brother's place.' In the way of men unused to the company of women, he whipped a battered hat from his dark head in an embarrassed afterthought. Hair almost as black as Tana's own tumbled over his forehead.

She took a deep breath and looked down quickly. Zachary Chase still had a weakening effect on her emotions that reminded her of feelings she'd had for him years before, the feelings of a teenager she thought she had outgrown. She had hoped that time in the city would introduce her to an entirely different kind of man; that she would lose forever that juvenile attraction to the rough and tumble types who populated the western ranges. But she had found nothing appealing whatsoever about the well-heeled men who scurried about cement cities in tailored suits. True, they didn't practise that domineering chauvinism that was a way of life out here; but they'd sacrificed something basic in the transition. Something male. Tana had found them all incredibly boring.

'The offer still stands, Tana.' She glanced up to find his dark eyes drilling hers, his broad shoulders tense beneath his heavy buckskin jacket. 'It's taken a lot of years, and almost all my savings, but I've got over two thousand acres now. It's good land. Together, we could make a good life on it.' His eyes narrowed as he studied her face, trying to read her thoughts. 'The last time I asked you to marry me, you ran away to the city.' His jaw tightened at the recollection of her rejection. 'I told you then that you didn't belong there, and you know that now, don't you? You didn't come back just for your dad's funeral. You came back to stay.' He nodded, as if her answer were unnecessary. 'So stay. You can't save this place, but you can share mine.'

She looked down at her hands and spoke steadily. 'It's too soon, Zach. I need time to think.'

He walked over and took her gently by the shoulders; under the steady pressure of his strong hands she felt a sudden, sharp awareness of his physical superiority, and for some reason that made her afraid. 'That's all right. I've waited six years already. I can wait another week. We'll talk about it when I get back.'

She lifted her head and searched his black eyes, retreating mentally because they were so hard to read. Did he love her? He'd never mentioned it, not even the first time he'd proposed, when she was only eighteen. Was that the reason she had turned away from the earthy, primitive attraction he held for her? Was it the reason she hesitated now?

'I hope your brother feels better soon,' she said quietly.

Zach sighed, dropped his hands from her shoulders, and snatched his hat from a nearby table. 'He picked a damn poor time to break his leg. I wish I didn't have to leave, but I'll be back as soon as I can arrange for someone else to manage his place while he's laid up.'

'It's all right, Zach. Take as long as you need.'

He nodded once, then walked towards the door, turning back at the last moment. He looked almost invincible, framed in the doorway with his legs slightly spread, his thumbs hooked in the front pockets of his jeans, his hat pulled low on his forehead, shading his eyes. 'Think about it, Tana. We could have a good life together.'

Her facial features sagged slightly as she heard the front door close behind him.

'Well, thank heavens *he's* gone.' The rasping voice belonged to Hazel, a rather large woman who had always been more family member than housekeeper. In the way of women who carried too much weight, her physical appearance had never seemed to change

over the years, and as she walked across the room
from the doorway Tana noted that her face was still
smooth and unlined. She had kind brown eyes that
reflected constant understanding, and a tiny little
mouth perched over a generous double chin. Only a
few strands of grey in the brown braid twisted on top
of her head marked the passage of time. Tana loved
her completely.

'You're too hard on Zach, Hazel. He's been a good
foreman.'

'I know that.' The older woman made no attempt to
conceal the hostility in her voice. She and Zach had
always clashed like two pieces of flint, although
neither one of them could ever explain why.

'He kept the ranch going all by himself while Dad
was bedridden. Even after all the other hands left. We
owe him a lot.'

'I know that, too,' Hazel grumbled.

The pick-up truck roared to life outside, and Tana
smiled a little wistfully, thinking that Zach drove a
truck the way he rode a horse—the way he did everything—fast, hard, and fearlessly.

'You've still got feelings for him, haven't you?'
Hazel's tone disapproved whatever she saw in Tana's
face. 'Just like when you were a teenager.'

'Don't be silly, Hazel,' she replied quickly. Too
quickly. 'I outgrew that sort of thing long ago. It's just
that I wish he didn't have to go right now, when I
need him most.'

'Hmph. Need him for what?'

Tana took a deep breath and steeled herself for an
explosion. 'I've decided, Hazel,' she said quietly. 'I've
got to go up there, find those cattle, and bring them

back down.'

Hazel's eyes almost disappeared in a narrow squint. She walked over to cradle Tana's chin in a large hand that smelled of flour, and there was a gentle scold in her frown. 'Don't be foolish, child. You'd be lucky to find that dinky little bunch of cows up there, let alone bring them down by yourself. What's got into you?'

Tana smiled faintly, then walked back towards the window. 'It's not just any bunch of cows, Hazel. It's Pillar. That bull made this ranch, and his spring calves would pay the debts on this place, and you know it.'

'Tana.' Hazel's voice was gentle. 'Even if you could get those cows down here to winter, what makes you think D.C. will wait until spring? They've been trying to foreclose for months, you know.'

Tana nodded at the cloud—bank building to the west. 'They might not have any choice. I phoned Judge Clark this morning. They can't start a foreclosure hearing until we've been served with the papers, and there's no way they'll get papers out here after that storm hits. Not until spring, anyway. By then we'll have enough money from the calves to make the back payments.'

'If we *have* any calves.'

'We'll have calves, Hazel,' Tana said softly.

Hazel lowered her bulk into a chair by the desk and sighed. 'You can't do it. I won't let you do it. It's too dangerous.'

Tana walked back to the desk, eased into her father's leather chair and drummed her fingers on the arms, a little confused by her own decision to risk the ride up to the high pastures. 'I have to go, Hazel.

If there's any chance at all of saving this place, I have to try, and don't ask me why, because I don't understand it myself.' She raised her head and was surprised to find Hazel smiling at her.

'I don't have to ask you why, child,' she said softly. 'You're a Mitchell, just like your daddy. Fighting back was bred into you, just like your black hair and those long Mitchell legs. But this is one time when you're going to have to walk away from the fight. You just can't risk riding up there alone.'

'Father would have done it,' Tana said quietly.

'Your father *did* it!' Hazel came back sharply, her voice filled with grief. 'And that's what killed him, in the end!'

The truth echoed in the silent room. It had been almost a year since Everett Mitchell's horse had thrown him on a lonely ride up to the summer pastures. He'd been bedridden ever since while his shattered legs healed, but the day he'd left his bed, less than one week ago, a residual blood clot from that very fall had loosened and struck him down.

Hazel leaned back in her chair and looked down at her hands while conflicting emotions moved across her face. 'You're going anyway, no matter what I say, aren't you?' she asked, quiet now.

'I have to, Hazel.'

Hazel's head bobbed in weary resignation, acknowledging what she had known all along. The funny thing was that, of the two women in the room, Hazel was the one who understood that sometimes a body had to take risks, and some things were worth taking risks for. This ranch was one of them, even though she suspected that Tana didn't fully realise that yet. Her bravado was only a knee-jerk reaction, but some day—some day when she made her peace with this place, she'd understand the real value of what she was fighting for now.

'I'd better pack some saddlebags for you,' she said gruffly, rising from the chair with a grace that belied her size. 'And I'll get on the phone, too. It isn't likely, but maybe there are still some travelling hands around, willing to sign on for the winter in exchange for bed and board. If I find anyone, I'll send them up to the first line-shack. You'll have to spend the night there, anyway. But you'll have to hurry, girl. That storm is coming on fast.' Suddenly her strong face crumpled and she had to press a hand quickly to her forehead to regain her composure. 'You ride slow, and you be careful, you hear?' she commanded. 'You haven't done any serious riding for years, and if you do find that bull, he might not remember you. You watch your back.'

Tana grabbed her hand and pressed it to her cheek. 'I'll be safer up there than I ever was in Chicago, Hazel. And Pillar will remember me. Bulls never forget.'

CHAPTER TWO

BY THE time Hazel stood watching Tana ride up the first of the slopes that rolled up to the Big Snowies, the sky was already a sickly shade of purple. Off in the distance, just topping the distant peaks, the dirty white underbelly of an enormous cloud-bank loomed ominously.

But the sky didn't bother Tana; nor did the biting wind that played with the open flaps of her sheepskin jacket. She felt the surging power of a good horse beneath her, smelled the clean crispness of coming snow in the air, and as far as she could see in any direction except behind her, man had made no mark on this wilderness. Good lord, had she really missed this all these years? Was that the explanation for the strained muscles in her face that finally let her know she'd been smiling for the better part of an hour?

She let Clancey, a big, steady horse the same colour as her hair, pick his own way along the trail, knowing he would head unerringly for the first line-shack. The reins hung loose while her body rolled automatically in response to the ground-covering jog, and for the first time since her father's funeral her mind was very nearly empty, occupied with nothing more serious than an absent recording of the scenery around her.

There were brown-eyed Susans drying in the early winter chill, the stemmy remains of goldenrod clustered like fading, ageing pom-pom girls beside the trail, and an endless expanse of emptiness that was oddly comforting. Everett Mitchell had died last week, and still life went on: the world looked the same; the mountains prevailed. There's something wrong with that, Tana thought sadly; and yet there's something right about it, too.

Eventually the twisting trail became steeper, dodging huge boulders scattered behind by some indifferent glacier aeons ago, and Clancey slowed his steady pace to a careful walk. Behind and beneath them the ranch became a speck in the distance, then disappeared altogether.

The incline of the trail broke often upon vast plateaux as flat as tables, perched on the hillside like a series of enormous stairs leading ever upwards. Here the forage was dried from early frosts, but still plentiful. Thousands of cattle could summer on these innumerable rich pastures, and the thought of searching for one bull and a few cows in such an endless wilderness made Tana shake her head in futile exasperation. There had been a time, years ago, when she had known every trick, every favourite hiding place of the old bull she'd made a pet when he was still a calf; but maybe Hazel was right. Maybe she was crazy to think that he hadn't changed his habits or his affectionate nature in the intervening years. Maybe she'd never find him; and maybe, if she did, he'd lower his head and charge.

The air had been growing steadily colder as she climbed, and the wind had freshened to a biting chill that smelled of imminent snow. Tana felt the first complaint from legs now more used to the tennis court than the blood-stilling confines of a saddle's stirrups. She breathed a sigh of relief when her horse rounded a sharp curve in the trail that brought her within a few hundred yards of the first line-shack.

It was a small, weathered, wooden structure squatting on the very top of the ridge, leaning as if to peer over the edge. A rickety paddock butted up to the east side of the shack, and Clancey whinnied when he saw it, recognising a place that held memories of feed and rest.

'Tired, aren't you, Clancey?' Tana murmured, slapping the muscular black neck affectionately. 'Me, too.'

She winced as she dismounted heavily, remembering the primitive fireplace inside the old building and the rock-hard cots where she would spend the night. She was a long way from her cosy lakeside apartment in Chicago, a long way from the well-heated classrooms where well-dressed college students frowned and slept through her lectures on American history; and suddenly she wasn't entirely sure what she was doing here.

The storm stalled on the western side of the mountains while Tana slept, and it was mid-morning by the time the first stinging pellets of dry snow began to fall.

I've gone soft, she was telling herself as she brushed Clancey down before saddling him. City life has made me soft.

Muscles she didn't remember having had locked in complaint when she'd tumbled out of the cot, a full two hours past the dawn that would have found any

self-respecting range-hand up and working. Worse
yet, the fire had burned down during the night, and so
spoiled was she by six years of electric ranges and
microwave ovens that it took her nearly half an hour
to get it going again. She was cold and stiff and
miserable, and just in the middle of wondering why
she was risking life and limb to save a way of life she
hated, when Clancey whickered and lifted his head.

Tana ducked her head to peep beneath his neck, and
a smile of relief lifted her features when she saw the
familiar stout shape of Mac, her father's favourite
horse, picking his way carefully over to the paddock.

'Oh, thank heavens,' she murmured, dropping her
brush, rushing over to the fence to grin up at the
strange rider. Long strands of her hair whipped in the
wind that played viciously with the air currents
surging up from the valleys below. She pushed it
impatiently away from her face, raising her voice to be
heard over the steady howl of the coming storm.

'I was just about to head east,' she shouted. 'There's
a cluster of flat pastures just beyond that ridge there,'
she pointed to a jutting rise about two miles distant,
'and if I know Pillar, that's where he'd head in a
storm.'

She climbed through the board fence and walked
right up to Mac's side, then peered up to get a look at
the face beneath the hat. 'I don't know who you are,
but am I ever glad to see you.' She hesitated, then
grinned. '*If* I could see you, that is.' She touched the
top of her own bare head, and in response the rider
pushed his hat back from over his eyes.

For a moment Tana thought the wind had stopped,
because suddenly everything seemed very quiet. Her

grin faded as she looked up into steady blue eyes that locked on to hers, commanding her full attention.

I would have known him anywhere, she thought, unconsciously catching her lower lip between her teeth. On the people-packed streets of Chicago, in a classroom, in the thick, smoky air of a crowded night-club . . . anywhere at all, I could have looked into those eyes and known instantly who he was, and what he was, and where he belonged.

It took her a moment to assimilate the rest of his features—the broad, smooth forehead marked by the faint ridge between light brows common to men who frowned more than they smiled, the wisps of thick blond flattened under the brim of his hat, contrasting sharply against the fading tan of summer sun and wind; the strong, lean angles of a face that looked hungry and angry all at the same time; the tight set of a mouth that looked grimly determined—but all of these things only confirmed what she had already known from the eyes.

His face reminded her of the old sepia photos of mountain men she'd seen in a dozen history books: men who lived in the wild and pitted their own strength against nature, the most formidable opponent of them all.

He belonged here, in these mountains, on this land, under this sky, more than any man she had ever seen. For a man who looked the way he did, any other life would have been too easy.

'Who's Pillar?' he asked suddenly, and even though he hadn't raised his voice she could hear it easily over the wind.

She blinked once, in confusion, as if she had never

expected him to speak—only to sit there on Mac's back like a living slice of history. Her thoughts scrambled for a foothold. Pillar—had she mentioned Pillar? Of course she had. But why didn't he know about the old bull?

'He's the bull we're up here to find,' she said, mystified. 'Didn't Hazel tell you that?'

He pulled his hat downwards over his brow before the wind could catch it, and crossed his arms over the saddle horn. 'Hazel . . . big lady, brown braid, voice like a chainsaw?'

Tana nodded and smiled.

'All she told me was that Everett Mitchell's fool of a daughter was up here alone,' he said stonily. 'Wasn't time to say much after that.'

Tana took a step backwards, her jaw tightening in typical Mitchell stubbornness. 'I see. Came racing up here to save the damsel in distress, did you?'

He bent his head so she couldn't see his face, touching the gloved fingers of one hand to his brow as if he'd forgotten why he'd come up here at all, and was trying to bring it back to mind. 'Not exactly,' he said finally, lifting his head, meeting her eyes again. 'Well . . . maybe. So why don't you finish saddling that horse and we'll get moving? We're going to have to ride hard enough as it is to beat this storm down.' He brushed the snowflakes from his gloved hands as if to emphasise his point.

Tana stood with her lips pressed into a grim line, her eyes flashing behind the strands of hair the wind tossed into her face. 'What are you talking about?' she finally shouted. 'We've got a bull and a hundred bred cows to find, and we're not going down until we do!

What do you think you've been hired for?'

'I haven't been hired,' he said flatly, and Tana grimaced in frustration.

'All right, so you aren't getting paid!' she snapped. 'But you are getting bunk and board for the winter, and apparently you agreed to that, or you wouldn't be here!'

'Bunk and board?' the man asked with a puzzled frown, lifting his hat from his head and slapping it against his thigh to shake off the snow.

Tana stared at the glorious shock of light hair that tumbled over his brow once it was released. Even tossed by the wind, the cut was obviously professional, something one didn't see often on a range-hand.

'That's right,' she said slowly, still staring at his hair, her dark brows almost touching in puzzlement. 'Bunk and board.' She shook her head quickly to clear it. 'But you won't get even that unless you're willing to work for it. Now, I'm heading over to those pastures beyond the ridge. If you want to go back down, fine. Go. But you go without me.'

Before he could reply she spun on her heel and ducked back through the paddock boards towards her horse. 'Are you out of your mind?' he called after her. 'Look around you! We're going to have the full force of this storm right here within the hour! There isn't a cow alive worth taking a risk like that!'

She stopped in the motions of slipping the bridle on Clancey and glared up at him. 'I'm not trying to save the cows,' she called over the wind. 'The cows are going to save me.'

She was the picture of confident determination as

she flung the blanket and then the saddle up on to Clancey's back, tightened the cinch, then swung up into the padded seat; but, for all her bravado, her heart was hammering and her palms inside the suede gloves were slick with sweat. She didn't know everything about these mountains, but she knew enough to be afraid to ride them alone.

She urged Clancey through the paddock gate and off towards the eastern ridge, and sighed with relief when she saw Mac follow out of the corner of her eye.

CHAPTER THREE

THE first part of the trail from the line-shack to the eastern pastures was narrow and rocky, and by necessity they rode single-file. Communication was impossible. Although straggly pines on either side of the beaten path provided some sort of protection from the wind-driven snow, the wind howled through with an increasing force that snatched words from their mouths and flung them away before they could be heard.

Tana glanced back occasionally, just to assure herself that the hostile range-hand was still behind her. Hostile or not, having someone, anyone, on the trail with her was a great comfort. Even with the added danger of the worsening weather, she was much more confident now than she had been alone yesterday.

She was still nervous leading the way, and every muscle in her body ached, but at least her worst fear was banished. If she should fall from the saddle and break a leg, or worse, someone would be there to pick her up. Someone competent and strong; someone used to hours in the saddle and the vagaries of Montana weather and the ever-present dangers of these hilly trails. It was almost like riding out with her father, trusting her life to him completely.

She smiled at the unintentional comparison,

because this tall, grim man certainly did not resemble her father. Nor did he resemble any of the men she had met in Chicago. He confirmed her belief that there was something special about men who disdained the world of technology and chose to live alone in what wilderness was left. Something hard and irresistibly masculine. More than anyone else, he reminded her of Zach; of the way she had thought she felt about Zach once, a very long time ago.

She straightened quickly, surprised at the turn her thoughts had taken. She had too much to do to be bothered with a childish attraction to a man right now. Giving in to such a thing, even briefly, was a real danger in the present situation.

After nearly an hour's ride, the narrow trail broke abruptly on to a wide plain and Tana pulled up her horse sharply, biting her lower lip at the scene before her. The trees, scattered though they had been, had done more than protect them from the biting wind; they had concealed the true fury of the storm that was certainly upon them.

Then plateau's tall, dried grasses were bent to the ground, frosted now with driving snow that had become sticky and wet. If this kept up, the plain would be impassable within a few hours. There was absolutely no hope of finding evidence of Pillar and the cows once a blanket of white covered any possible clues, and Tana's shoulders slumped in despair.

The range-hand eased Mac up beside Clancey, and the trail was so narrow at this point that his knee scraped against hers. Tana felt the warmth of his leg beneath his heavy jeans, and took a sharp breath.

'Good lord,' he murmured, shaking his head, staring out across the windswept plain. He lifted his hat from his head and ran his fingers back through hair already damp with snow. 'This is hopeless. You ready to give it up now?'

'It's not as bad as it looks,' she said quickly, turning to look at him with a plea in her eyes. 'You can't see it through the snow, but this field isn't that broad. Only an eighth of a mile or so. On the other side, there's a natural tunnel through the ridge that leads to the pastures. They're pretty well sheltered from the west, so it should be better over there.'

He stared at her thoughtfully, the bright blue of his eyes softened by the day's unnatural darkness. 'Even if the cattle are there, we'd never be able to get them back this way. The snow will be too deep by the time we get them rounded up, and they'd never manage this narrow trail. As I said, it's hopeless, and you know it, too. I can hear it in your voice.'

'There's another way down,' she said desperately. 'From that side. It's steeper, but not as narrow, and it's a shorter route back to the ranch. Wouldn't take more than three hours to lead them down.'

The man grunted and slapped his hat back on his head, pulling the brim down low. 'We don't have three hours,' he said flatly. 'It'll be dark early in this storm. It isn't getting any better, in case you hadn't noticed, and it's going to get a lot worse. This is just the leading edge.'

'We'll spend the night in the pastures, then start down in the morning.' There was a hard, frantic edge to her voice.

'If the cows are there.'

'If the cows are there,' she repeated quietly.

'And if I went back to the shack, you'd just go ahead without me, wouldn't you?' he asked, angry again.

She pressed her lips together and tasted snow. 'I'd have to,' she said decisively, hardly able to believe her lips had managed to form the words. Would she really? Was she really capable of such foolish courage?

Apparently he believed she was, because he nodded once, as if she had just confirmed something he'd already known, then squeezed his legs gently against Mac's sides, moving the bay horse forward, leading the way.

The full force of the wind hit them the moment they moved away from the shelter of the tree-lined trail, and they both grabbed for their hats, pulling them down until they were painfully tight against their foreheads. They hunched into the collars of their sheepskin jackets and bent forward over their horses' necks, giving the wind as small a target as possible; but still the stinging smack of driven snow found their cheeks, and the chill blew right through the smallest gap between clothing and skin.

Over the hunched shoulders of the man who led her, Tana searched for a dark blotch ahead that would mark the ridge of rock they were headed for. After fifteen minutes it materialised just a few feet ahead, and both horses picked up the pace, sensing shelter in the tunnel nature had carved through the rock to the pastures beyond.

Once safely inside the shelter of rock, the horses stopped of their own accord, blowing steam noisily from their nostrils, shaking off the snow that had frozen in clumps to their manes. Their riders both swept their hats from their heads, shaking out their hair, and then their eyes met in a curious, tingling camaraderie.

Tana smiled at him timidly, her cheeks bright red from the cold and glistening with moisture from melted snow. 'I know this sounds ridiculous,' she said, 'but I feel like a kid at camp. I haven't done this sort of thing in years.'

There was a strange exhilaration in the blue eyes that Tana could feel shining from her own; the kind of exhilaration that came from matching your strength to an opponent's, and winning.

'Defying death and danger?' he asked wryly. 'That sort of thing?'

She laughed nervously, heard the echo in the sudden quiet of the wind-free tunnel, then lowered her voice to a whisper. 'I know it sounds stupid, especially to someone who does this sort of thing for a living, but I haven't done anything the least bit risky since I left the ranch years ago. I'd forgotten how good it could feel. Even the bad parts, even being afraid—sometimes even that feels good.' She laughed again. 'Especially when it's over.'

'It isn't over,' he reminded her. 'And I'd hold back on all those good feelings, if I were you. What if the cattle you're so desperate to find aren't in these pastures? What then?'

She shrugged and looked away. 'They will be,' she said a little uncertainly. 'And if not, I'll keep looking. As long as I can.'

He took a deep breath and scowled at her. 'You haven't worked this ranch in years?'

Tana felt the guilt close around her. 'It wasn't my dream. It was my father's. I could hardly wait to get away from it.'

'And what was your dream?'

She opened her mouth to answer automatically, then closed it slowly. 'I don't know. I'm not sure I ever had one.'

He was lacing the ends of his reins in a braid, watching his hands work the leather. 'Well, I'm glad to hear this ranch wasn't it.'

'Why?'

He jerked his head up, as if he'd said too much, and was waiting for her to catch him at the mistake. 'Because you don't know what you're doing, that's why,' he said gruffly.

Tana looked directly into the contemptuous blue eyes for a long moment, then turned away. On rare occasions in her life she had felt an unfamiliar spark of defiance, a stubborn streak she barely recognised in herself, and on those occasions she took offence easily and lashed out. But life hadn't prepared her to stand up for herself often—she'd always had someone else to do that for her. So it was that she let his disdainful remark pass, even though she suspected he would think less of her for it.

'You don't have to tell me that I don't know what I'm doing up here,' she said softly. 'No one knows that better than I do. I never had anything to do with running this ranch, but I'm afraid the ranch doesn't have any choice this time. My father died last week; all the hands left long ago, when the money ran out, and I'm the only one left.'

'I'm sorry,' he said quickly, sounding as genuinely apologetic as if the whole mess was somehow his fault.

'It's all right.' She shrugged, pretending a courage

she didn't feel. 'There's still a chance, if I can just get these cattle down into the valley for the winter . . .'

'Hold it.' He was shaking his head, holding up one hand to stop her in mid-sentence. 'You don't have to tell me all this,' he said gruffly. 'It's your business, not mine.'

'No, it's your business, too. You're risking a lot, coming up here, helping me out, knowing you might not get anything for your trouble but a place to winter. You have a right to know . . .'

'But I don't want to know!' he shouted unexpectedly.

Tana jerked back in her saddle, her eyes wide. He glared at her stricken expression for a moment.

'Oh, hell!' he grumbled finally, squeezing Mac's sides hard with his legs until the horse surged forwards. 'Forget it. Let's take a look for those mythical cattle of yours. If they aren't in the pastures ahead, at least we'll have time to get back down to the ranch before full night.'

Tana let her horse follow his through the short tunnel while she kept her eyes riveted to the long, straight back. There had been no reason at all for his sudden outburst, and it had almost startled her into tears. The man was a total mystery, even for a range-hand. For a moment there he had seemed almost like a young boy, savouring the ride and the danger and the mission as if it were all brand new; and then suddenly he'd become hostile, almost as if he had something against her personally.

The wind carried her confused sigh off to the east as they emerged from the tunnel on to a steep slope that dropped to the pastures below. Half-way down the slope the ridge formed a natural windbreak, and the driving snow lessened enough for Tana to pause and peer downwards to the grassy table.

'Pillar!' she cried joyfully, and the range-hand reined Mac to a halt and followed her gaze.

The pasture below was sheltered from the worst of the storm, and tall, brittle grasses still stood straight, barely dusted with snow. Scattered across the dried meadow were the squat red and white forms of Hereford cattle, grazing nonchalantly, unconcerned at the storm that raged hundreds of feet above them.

'I told you! I told you!' she cried, bouncing up and down in the saddle happily. 'Look at him, that old, gorgeous brute! He knew just where to go!'

And then she was kicking her horse's sides, speeding down the rocky slope heedlessly, leaving little slides of stony dirt in her wake. The man she left behind shook his head slowly and followed at a more dignified pace, then urged Mac to a faster gait when he saw Tana reach the basin and gallop towards the enormous, muscled animal that had to be the bull.

'Are you crazy?' he shouted, pushing Mac to a gallop when he reached the bottom. 'That's a bull, not a puppy! Get away from him?'

But Tana never heard him, and by the time he had closed the distance between them to a hundred yards, she had already slid from her saddle and was running up to the bull's side.

His face twisted in a fearful grimace as he watched the bull raise its massive, short-horned head and face the young woman running towards him. Billows of steam rose from the challenging snorts of the brute's nostrils.

Suddenly the animal sagged from his initial, tense posture of challenge to a stance of complacency, and Tana threw her arms around his thick neck and buried her face into the heavy winter coat. The bull not only tolerated this, he actually seemed to enjoy it. He lifted his heavy head and tipped it to one side as she scratched between his horns, and closed both eyes in a languid blink of obvious pleasure.

'Well, I'll be damned,' the range-hand muttered from a few yards away, jerking back in the saddle when his voice made the bull raise his head abruptly at the strange voice.

Tana laughed, rubbing hard at the bony head. 'It's OK, Pillar,' she told the vicious-looking beast. 'He's just a man, just like Dad. Not another bull at all.' She laughed again when she saw light brows lift slightly as the man wondered whether or not he'd been insulted.

'I raised him from a calf,' she explained, looking up happily. 'No one could ever understand why I got so attached to a stupid bull, but Pillar was always different. Smarter than most, and almost affectionate. Other kids had dogs; I had a bull.'

The man shifted his weight in the saddle, obviously still wary of putting both feet on the ground within charging distance of the massive animal. 'OK,' he said slowly, 'so now what? You've got almost a hundred cows in this field, and though it's sheltered enough for now, by tomorrow the storm is going to drop this far. Then what? How do you think the two of us are going to round them up and get them all down?'

Tana gave the bull one last pat and returned to her horse. 'Oh, we won't have to round them up,' she said matter-of-factly. 'I'll just put a rope around Pillar's neck and lead him down. The cows will follow.'

'Really,' he said drily. 'And what makes you think old Pillar is going to tolerate being led around like a dog?'

She climbed into her saddle and smiled and frowned at him all at once. 'He's still just a baby at heart,' she replied, and then trotted away towards the sheltered side of the field.

'Baby, my foot,' he muttered sceptically at the huge bull, noting the wide horn-span, the deep, muscular chest.

Pillar raised his head with a trumpeting snort, and the man kicked Mac into a canter and sped away.

CHAPTER FOUR

TANA had headed for a small grove of spruce trees that clustered at the base of the ridge like children huddled around their mother's skirt. By the time the man cantered up, she had already dismounted and was loosening the cinch of her horse's saddle.

'How bad is the trail from here down to the ranch?' he asked her.

She could hear the worry in his voice, and saw it confirmed in his eyes as they scanned the quickly darkening sky.

'It's getting worse, isn't it?'

He nodded sombrely. 'Up there, it is. The cold air might keep it stalled up on the peaks for a while, or it might just drop down on us like a bomb, depending on how far the temperature falls. You know these mountains. You can never really tell how much time you have.'

'I know,' she answered in a small voice, feeling the spirit of adventure seeping away as a cold knot of anxiety crawled into its place. 'The trail is broad enough, and the slope isn't too steep, but it's loose rock most of the way down. There are a lot of wash-outs. I don't think I'd want to try it in the dark.'

He nodded thoughtfully, his expression calm, then slipped from the saddle with a practised sweep of his leg. He led Mac into the trees, closer to Tana's horse, until he was standing right next to her. She stared up at him for a moment in surprise. He was much taller than she'd thought he was.

'Not a bad spot,' he said absently, looking at his surroundings. The pines made a natural shelter backed up to the wall of rock, with boughs laced together in a fragrant roof just a few feet over their heads. Years of discarded needles carpeted the ground beneath them. He removed his hat, banging it on his thigh to shake off the snow, then hung it from the stub of a bough high on the closest tree. 'You camp here often?'

'Only once. The hands did all the stock-running from the summer pastures, but Dad brought me up here when I was a kid for my first night on the ground. An initiation, of sorts.'

'We'll need a fire tonight,' he said thoughtfully, pulling the cinch through the large metal ring, his hands acting automatically. 'It might not do much to keep us warm, but at least it'll keep the cattle from trampling us during the night. It's my guess that they'll head right for these trees if the storm drops this low.'

Tana watched him surreptitiously over the neck of her horse, feeling secret relief at having an experienced hand here to think of all the things that might never have occurred to her.

He stripped the saddle from Mac's back, rubbing his gloved hand vigorously over the flattened hair beneath, paying particular attention to where the girth had been cinched under the belly. Tana did the same for her own horse, remembering her father's cardinal rule about treating your horse as if it were the only

lifeline you had to the outside world. It was a range
rule that still held true; particularly on a night like
tonight.

She dug in her saddlepack for the small portion of
grain that would serve her horse on the trail, and
watched him do the same; then they both attached
hobbles to their horses' legs to keep them close to
camp for the night.

'I'll gather some wood while you make a spot for the
fire. Over there, I think, away from the trees a little,
but not too far in the open. We'll need plenty of pine
needles to get it started.'

Tana nodded and watched him walk deeper into the
grove of trees, realising for the first time that she was
about to spend the night with a stranger. There was
absolutely nothing erotic about the situation, of
course; or about her either, for that matter. Men
might look excitingly rugged in the clothes of the
range, but there was nothing especially appealing
about a female dressed for a winter night in a sleeping-
bag.

She looked down a little sadly at her own garb—
heavy jeans with thick, long underwear beneath, and a
sheepskin jacket over two sweaters and a wool shirt—
and wished that she were dressed a little differently.

Her conscious inventory of her clothes made her
think of the rest of her appearance, and her hands flew
to her head. She moaned aloud when she felt the
tangled disarray of her long hair; tried to comb it into
some semblance of order with cold-stiffened fingers,
then swore aloud and dropped her hands. She didn't
need a mirror to know it was hopeless, and what was
she thinking of, anyway? She hadn't come up here

to entice a strange bed-and-board hand. She had a job to do, and she didn't need a comb or make-up to get it done.

By the time he returned with an armload of dried branches, she had already prepared the fire pit, and had unloaded the food from both sets of saddlebags. She held up a can in each hand. 'Pork and beans, or beef stew?'

He looked off into the distance with a hint of a smile.

'Well?'

He turned his head slowly and smiled down at her, and she was startled by the sheer beauty of his face while it was wearing that particular expression. 'Pork and beans,' he said softly. 'I'd like that.' Then he dropped to his knees before the fire pit and began to shred kindling from the branches with quick, sure flashes of a small pocket-knife.

Tana stared at his back for a long time after he'd turned, her lips parted slightly, her brows cocked in a puzzled frown. There was something decidedly odd about a range-hand who could be that moved by the prospect of pork and beans.

She opened two large cans with the can opener hooked on to her belt, and set them close to the fire that was just beginning to send up tendrils of smoke. They'd tuck the cans deep into the coals when they got hot enough, and her mouth was already watering at the thought of hot food. She hadn't had a bite since breakfast in the line-shack, and assumed he hadn't either.

'Hey,' she said suddenly, sitting back on her heels. 'I just realised that I don't even know your name.'

He leaned away from the fire, then turned his head towards her slowly. Tana's eyes narrowed suspiciously when she realised he was reluctant to tell her his name. That probably meant he was a rouge—one of those volatile cowhands with a history of trouble that followed them from ranch to ranch, keeping them solitary, and for the most part unemployed.

'Don't worry about it,' she said with a wry smile. 'I've been away from the grapevine for so long that I don't know who the undesirables are any more. I don't care who you worked for last, or what kind of trouble you got into there. And even if I did, what would I do? Fire you and hire one of others waiting in line?'

She expected him to smile, but he didn't.

'Cody,' he said quietly, watching her face carefully for a reaction. 'Douglas Cody.'

She stuck out a gloved hand, and for some reason he winced a little as he took it. 'Well, Cody, it's a pleasure to meet you. I guess I should have said that earlier. As it turns out, finding this herd wasn't as difficult as it might have been, and even getting them down to the ranch might be easy; but feeding and caring for a hundred head over the winter would be too much for Hazel and me. I'm glad you signed on, and I promise that somehow, some day, I'll make it worth your while.'

He turned away and took a deep breath. 'Actually, I hadn't planned to stay the winter.'

'Oh.' She frowned at his sudden coldness, then shrugged it away as one of the expected eccentricities of a range-hand unused to the company of others —women, in particular.

'I'm sorry,' she said quietly. 'I guess I was assuming a lot. Anyone who takes a bunk-and-board job this late in the season is usually looking for a place to winter.'

There was an uncomfortable silence between them for a long moment, then Tana inched closer to the fire, and by necessity closer to him.

'I don't suppose this is very pleasant for you,' she said.

'What do you mean by that?'

She flinched at the sharp suspicion in his tone. 'I just meant . . . being out in weather like this; having to spend the night half-way up a mountain with a woman you don't even know.'

He almost laughed out loud. 'I never object to spending the night with a woman,' he said without thinking, then jerked his head quickly to look at her round eyes and lifted brows. 'I didn't mean that exactly the way it sounded,' he hedged quickly.

Tana chuckled. 'Don't apologise, Cody,' she said easily, automatically giving his last name first-name status, as was common in this part of the country. 'I was brought up around range-hands, and I'd guess that you meant exactly what you said.' Her smile was almost mischievous. 'And I'd be willing to bet that a man like you has a long trail of broken hearts behind him,' she went on blithely, unzipping her jacket to the fire's warmth. She blushed as his eyes dropped to the ripe curves even several layers of clothing couldn't conceal, and wondered if perhaps she hadn't carried this particular conversation much too far already.

'We'd better get those in the fire.' She nodded towards the opened cans.

He turned away long enough to place the cans on

the coals, then turned back, frowning. 'Sorry about that,' he said brusquely.

'Sorry about what?' she asked with feigned innocence, more comfortable pretending ignorance than admitting she had seen the direction of his gaze.

His mouth quirked in a little smile. 'For noticing you're a woman, of course.'

Tana inhaled sharply, surprised by his directness. His laugh was spontaneous. 'And now I'm sorry I shocked you by stating the obvious. Tact never was one of my strong points.'

She felt her face grow hot with the rush of blood, then remembered where she was and laughed suddenly at her own pretence of civilisation. 'Oh, my,' she sighed happily, feeling delightfully free for the first time in years. 'I'm afraid I've been away from all this for too long. I'd almost forgotten what it's like to carry on a conversation with someone who doesn't wander all around the issue before he finally sneaks up on it. Straight talk, Dad used to call it. He said there wasn't time for any other kind out here. I'm just out of practice.'

'Your Dad must have been quite a man,' Cody said softly, staring into the fire.

'Oh, he was. Quite a man.' Tana gazed into the hypnotic flames, her nostrils flaring to capture the molasses-rich smell of warming beans, wondering why the sharp edge of grief dulled in the presence of this man; why it was suddenly more comfort than pain to think of her father. She smiled nostalgically as her memories brought him to life. 'He knew everything there was to know about this country, and about cattle,' she mused, oblivious to Cody's sudden attention. 'Started with ten cows when he bought this spread, and built the herd up to two thousand within ten years. And not two thousand scrubs, mind you, but sturdy, prize-winning pedigreed Herefords, every one. People came all the way from Texas to buy Dad's stock; Mexico, too. As a matter of fact,' she sighed sadly, 'this is the first year we've ever had to ship direct to the feedlots. In the old days, almost all the cattle were sold as breeding stock long before winter.'

Cody had been staring at her profile as she spoke, watching the reflected flicker of firelight play across creamy skin; but now he frowned, rethinking the words his subconscious had recorded. 'Two thousand head?' he asked, disbelieving. 'You were running two thousand head on this place?'

Tana glanced at him with heart-wrenching innocence. 'Sure. Why?'

'How long ago did you have that many cattle?' he asked with an abrupt impatience that was almost rude.

Tana cocked her head at the strange intensity in his voice. 'Well, as far as I know, we always had that many, up until my dad's accident last spring.' She closed her eyes briefly, remembering the awesome losses recorded in the old ledger. 'We lost nearly a thousand to disease during the drought last summer, then apparently Dad had to sell off a lot of them to make the grazing last, so now we only have these.'

'Tana,' he said tightly, using her name for the first time, 'that doesn't make sense. Even in the worst drought, this land could support two thousand head easily, let alone half that number. There's no way your father would have to cut the herd that drastically to make the grazing last. But even if he did ship that many, he should have made a pile of money on them. Beef prices were sky high this summer.'

Tana shrugged. 'He must have had a pile of debts to match,' she said sorrowfully, 'because there certainly isn't any money left now. He couldn't even make the payments on the ranch mortgage. That's why they're foreclosing.'

Cody dropped his eyes and clenched his jaw. 'Beans are bubbling,' he said, snatching a handkerchief from his pocket and reaching gingerly for the hot cans.

They ate in relative silence as they faced the little fire and the pasture beyond, the bean cans stuck into the frozen ground between their crossed legs.

'Put your biscuit on top of the can between bites,' he instructed her at one point. 'It'll keep the heat in the can, and thaw the biscuit, all at the same time.'

She followed his instructions doubtfully, then grinned when she bit into a biscuit almost as tender as when Hazel had pulled it from the oven. 'Hey, that's terrific. Now why didn't Dad ever tell me that?'

Cody tossed more of the small branches on the fire and huddled deeper into his jacket.

They could hear the howl of wind high above them on the ridge and, though they were relatively sheltered from the weather at a lower elevation, occasionally the pine boughs whistled a warning of worse to come. The cold dropped like a heavy blanket as soon as darkness fell, and by squinting past the fire across the field Tana could see that the snow was now falling thickly enough to accumulate. 'Pillar isn't going to like this,' she said, more to herself than to Cody.

'Pillar isn't the only one. I think it's time we got the

bags out.'

He unwrapped both sleeping-bags from their tidy bundles and stretched them out close to the fire. 'Take your boots off, and tuck them into the bottom of your bag.'

'Keeps them warm, right?' she asked, following his instructions.

'Warm in the winter, and snake-free in the summer.'

She nodded and inched her way into the cold sleeping-bag, shivering until her body heat warmed the tiny enclosure. She rolled on to her stomach and propped her chin on her hands, and studied the stranger next to her with unabashed interest.

He was tucked in his own bag, facing the fire, stretched out on one side with his head propped on his hand. The firelight laced his hair with threads of gold, and yellow sparks flickered in the blue of his eyes. The memory of a childhood doll popped into Tana's mind with the soft, sweet explosion of a happy recollection. It had been a magical, wondrous thing to her childish perceptions, with glassy blue eyes and strands of sparked gold for hair, and the difference between them had been a marvel. Could there be such blonde, blue-eyed lightness in a world that also produced her own dark hair and eyes? She hadn't thought so then, and for that reason that inanimate bit of fakery had been a constant source of fascination.

'This is fun, isn't it?' she said suddenly.

He turned disbelieving eyes on her, then laughed out loud. 'You're a wonder, lady.'

She shrugged and rolled on to her back, tucking her hands behind her head. 'Oh, you just don't understand. And why should you? You do this sort of thing all the time. It's part of your job. But for me . . . well, it's been a long time since I've been out here. Now I know why a man like you chooses this kind of life.'

'And what kind of a man am I?' Cody asked evenly, his eyes playing over her face.

'A loner,' she said certainly. 'The kind of man who doesn't need anybody else. Doesn't want anybody else.'

He pulled his eyes from her reluctantly and stared into the fire. 'You've been reading too many Western novels,' he said gruffly. 'That kind of man, or woman, doesn't exist. There's no such thing as a loner. Only someone who's been left alone. We all need somebody.'

She rolled on her side to face him, her eyes bright with curiosity. 'Even you?'

'Even me.'

'And do you have somebody?'

His lips curled in a half-smile. 'A woman, you mean? No, not at the moment. How about you? You have some snappy executive waiting for you out east?'

'No,' she answered softly, thinking that these were the preliminaries. Although the questions were casually innocent, the intent was not. She squirmed in her bag and frowned, suddenly uncomfortable.

'Cold?'

'A little,' she admitted, 'but I'd better get used to it. I imagine it'll get a lot colder before the night is over.'

'Move your bag closer to mine,' he ordered, and she stared at him uncertainly. 'Well, come on. I don't bite.'

'I know that,' she said shyly, dropping her eyes.

'I . . . just don't know you very well. Cuddling up to a complete stranger isn't something I do every day.'

'There are no strangers on the range,' he recited the old adage she'd heard her father say so often, and the familiar words sounded reassuring. She chided herself for being unnecessarily nervous, and moved awkwardly in the bag to sidle up next to him. Just the physical contact of another human being was comforting, and she snuggled up happily until the top of her head brushed his chin. It was just like snuggling up to Hazel, or her father, or any number of people who had filled her young life with the warmth of physical affection, and she was totally unaware that he had stiffened slightly.

'You sure you haven't done this before?' he whispered hoarsely, and she went immediately rigid, realising what she was doing.

'Oh, dear.' She jerked to a sitting position in the bag and blushed until her cheeks were bright red.

'No, no.' He pulled her back down until her head rested on his shoulder. 'I didn't mean to embarrass you. It's all right. Really. Relax.'

But it wasn't all right, and this wasn't like snuggling up to Hazel, or her father, or anyone else. Even as she eased back and let her head fall once again to his shoulder, she was telling herself to get up and run— not from Douglas Cody, necessarily, but from what he was making her feel. But, if she did that, then he'd *know* she was feeling it, and that would be worse.

She lay stiffly in the cradle of his arm, wondering what on earth was the matter with her. This was about as unromantic as life ever got, shivering beneath several layers of clothes in the face of a life-threatening blizzard, with the unmelodic bellows of a hundred restless cows as background music. So why wasn't she miserable? Why wasn't she concentrating on the icy wind, or her sore muscles, or the hard ground beneath her? Why was she only aware of the warmth of his shoulder under her cheek, the full, steady beat of his heart under her ear, the fresh-air smell of his neck, reflecting her own breath?

Her peripheral vision caught a glimpse of his left hand curled around her shoulder, and that, more than anything else, was disturbingly personal. Good lord. She was spending the night in the embrace of a man whose name she had only learned an hour ago.

She stirred against him and tipped her head to look up at his face, as if she would find the answer for her own feelings there, clearly written in the crystalline blue of his eyes. But what she saw made her suddenly afraid, although she couldn't have put a name to it.

As his gaze met hers, she felt the warning thump of his quickening heartbeat under her cheek, and felt her own flutter in response; then his eyes narrowed, somehow accusing her, and his nostrils flared briefly with the sharp pull of his breath. She opened her mouth to deny what was happening, or to stop it—she would never know which, because before she could speak, without any warning at all, he dropped his hand and brushed her lips with his. The contact was electrifying, and they both jerked away from it simultaneously, wide brown eyes meeting wide blue ones, mouths identically parted in an expression somewhere between shock and wonder.

He pushed her away abruptly and sat up.

Tana lay where she had tumbled when he pushed

her from him, one hand touching her lips. She imagined that she could still feel the heat of his mouth where it had touched her.

He reached for another branch and tossed it angrily into the fire, shooting pinwheels of sparks into the frosty air. 'I'm sorry,' he said gruffly, drawing his knees up inside the bag, draping his elbows across them, staring straight ahead into the flames.

'It's all right,' she said quietly, sitting up next to him, cocking her head so that she could watch his face from the side. 'It was only a kiss. There's nothing wrong with that.'

His laugh was short and hard. 'You have no idea just how much is wrong with that. And there's no such thing as "only a kiss".'

Tana stared at him, thinking that what he said was probably true—with this man, there would never be such a thing. Was that what had made it so different? Was that why she felt as if she'd just been kissed for the very first time?

Involuntarily, her mind replayed the first time Zachary had kissed her in the shadow of these very mountains. After a long string of meaningless kisses by a long line of clammy-palmed, urgent young men, Zachary had left her shaken. Part of it was because he'd made her feel the vague stirrings of what she imagined she was supposed to feel—but what had disturbed her most was the fanciful notion that the mountains had been watching, and that they didn't approve. Ridiculous fancy or not, she hadn't felt it with Cody, but that might have been simply because he'd taken her by surprise.

'I want to try it again,' she said abruptly.

'What?'

'Would you kiss me again?'

His head reared back on his shoulders and he looked at her in amazement. 'Why the hell would you want me to do that?'

She scrambled through her mind for a reason that made more sense than the real one, and smiled when she came up with one that had a validity all its own. 'Because I liked it. Didn't you?'

He said nothing for a moment; he just stared at her. Then he exhaled, shaking his head in disbelief. 'Are you really all that naïve? Look around you. You see anyone ready to rush to your rescue when things get out of hand?'

She straightened and frowned at him, baffled because he seemed angry. 'Things won't get out of hand . . .' she began, but before the last word was out of her mouth his voice was booming, reverberating across the meadow.

'How the hell do you know that?' he shouted, startling her so much that she jerked backwards, away from him. 'You don't know the first thing about me! What happens if I decide a kiss isn't enough? What happens if I decide to take more—to take *you*—whether you like it or not?'

Tana was speechless for a moment, her mouth and eyes three circles of definition in the pale wash of her face. 'I know you wouldn't do that,' she finally managed to whisper, and even as the words left her mouth, she wondered where her certainty came from.

'And that,' he jerked his head away with an expression of disgust, 'is probably why the Mitchells can't hang on to what's theirs. You're too damned trusting.'

Tana swallowed once, her body rigid, finally recovering enough presence of mind to reach inside for her own measure of anger. 'I don't trust everyone,' she snapped petulantly.

He whipped his head around to glare at her, and a shock of blonde tumbled over his brow and glittered in the firelight. 'But you trust *me*?' he shouted.

'Yes!' she shouted back without thinking, and then stilled because the admission astonished her as much as it did him. She did trust him, and that wasn't only foolish, it was incomprehensible. He was secretive, rude, and undeniably volatile, reacting to the simplest things with the most inexplicable anger, and yet she felt safer with him than she had ever felt in her life. She sat there for a moment and marvelled at her own idiocy, ascribing it, as she always did, to the worst of all possible evils: blind, deaf, dumb instinct.

He closed his eyes and shook his head, and she watched the anger drain out of his face. When he opened his eyes, there was a deep, quiet sorrow in the blue depths. 'It's the most dangerous thing in the world, you know,' he said quietly.

'What is?'

'Trust.'

She pressed her lips together thoughtfully. 'Shouldn't I trust you?'

'Hell, no, you shouldn't,' he grumbled, sliding down into his bag and then rolling pointedly away from her.

She stared at the hulking shape of his sleeping-bag for a time, then snuggled down into her own, rolling towards him so she could watch his back in the faint glow of the fire. She heard the wild whistle of the wind creeping down from the heights, and smiled. Tomorrow, the storm would lash the valley with its full fury, and, as it was every winter, the ranch would be cut off from the outside world. No one would be able to get in with a summons for a foreclosure hearing, and better yet—no one would be able to get out.

CHAPTER FIVE

'TANA.'

She snuggled deeper into the warmth of her sleeping-bag, jerking her shoulder away from the gentle press of insistent fingers.

'Tana. Miss Mitchell.'

She went rigid suddenly. There was something very wrong about being wakened by someone who called her Miss Mitchell. Her eyes flew open.

Cody was kneeling next to her, his face hovering above hers, his mouth slashing the rough stubble of a beard several shades darker than his hair. 'A man could make a career out of waking you up. Do you always sleep so soundly?'

The deep, rumbling tones of his voice relaxed her, and she rolled on to her back and stretched the cramps out of her legs, smiling up at him through a yawn. 'Is it morning already?'

The delicious lethargy of lingering sleep, those precious few seconds before the inhibitions of civilised behaviour were fully awake, made her reach out with one hand to touch his cheek. She grinned at the rough bristles beneath her fingers. 'You need a shave.'

He jerked back, surprised at her touch, and that underlined the intimacy of her gesture.

'I'm sorry,' she stammered, fully awake now, and

completely embarrassed. What on earth had made her do such a thing? She jerked to a sitting position in the sleeping-bag, staring down at the hand that had touched him as if it were someone else's, doing things she couldn't control. Suddenly the sound of wind and the bite of cold made her look up and take in her surroundings. 'Oh, dear,' she murmured, her words barely a sigh as her hand flew to her lips in surprise.

The grassy plateau of last night was now an ocean of white, sprouting its own bearded stubble where the two-foot blades poked only their dried heads through the snow. Off in the distance, the cattle were clustered in a tight flower of red and white, tails to the freshening wind, as still as if they had already been frozen in place. Heavy clouds hung in a rumpled blanket so close to the earth that there was barely a definition between land and sky. Snow fell like a curtain that divided their pine shelter from the world beyond.

'We have to leave!' she exclaimed, scrambling inside the bag for her boots, her voice edged with panic.

'Take it easy.' His voice was as soothing as his hand on her shoulder. 'I already grained the horses and packed up, except for your bag. We can get started as soon as you're ready. Here. No time for a hot meal this morning.' He handed her a stick of dried beef and a tin cup of snow that had been melted into warm water over the fire. Tana drank gratefully, then stuck the beef into her mouth like a cigar and gnawed on it as she pulled on her boots. Within moments she was fully dressed and her sleeping-bag was rolled into a compact cylinder, ready to be strapped on behind her saddle.

'I'll take care of that.' Cody took the roll from her and handed her the leather halter and rope she'd packed in her saddlebags. 'You sure that bull's going to let you do this?'

She jammed her hat on to her head, tied it down with a heavy wool scarf, then buttoned the wide collar of her jacket and pulled it up over her chin. 'I'm sure,' she mumbled through the sheepskin, taking the halter and rope. 'You'll bring the horses?'

Cody pulled his own hat down on his forehead and looked at her from under lowered brows. 'I'll be right behind you. Be careful.'

Tana cocked her head at the concern in his voice and smiled. 'Nice of you to worry about me.'

'Nothing personal,' he said gruffly, turning away.

Tana felt a sharp drop in temperature the moment she stepped away from the protection of the pines. The wind was steady, but tolerable—barely a breeze compared to what it would be in a few hours when the storm dropped even further. Good thing we're getting an early start, she thought as she ploughed through the deepening snow towards the cluster of cows. With any kind of luck at all, we should be back at the ranch with the herd settled in the loafing barn by lunchtime.

She felt a glimmer of apprehension as the cows stirred at her approach, a few of them bawling at the unwelcome intrusion of another creature within their tight circle of warmth. Cautiously, hands outstretched to touch the nearly wild creatures and move them aside, Tana made her way to where Pillar stood like a monarch in his proper place of honour, right in the centre of the herd. He lifted his heavy head, peered near-sightedly over the moist breadth of his nose, then bawled a challenge at the intruder. Immediately Tana spoke to him, one gloved hand outstretched, offering the sugar cube he had learned to expect as a calf, hoping he would remember. After a moment of heart-stopping hesitation, he nuzzled her palm, lipping the sweet morsel back on to his tongue, closing his eyes in his old, docile gesture of trust. He barely moved as she slipped the halter over his head, almost as if he anticipated the shelter and food that had always followed his willingness to submit.

Tana looked back over her shoulder and saw Cody guiding Mac carefully through the cows, leading Clancey by one rein. Already there was an inch of white powder icing his hat and shoulders, and his face was reddened by the cold.

'I never would have believed it if I hadn't seen it for myself,' Cody said, leaning sideways in the saddle to hand her Clancey's rein. 'Every range bull I ever knew would just as soon gore a man as look at him.'

Tana forced a tight smile, then busied herself brushing away the snow that clung to her jeans so he wouldn't see the strain in her face. When she finally climbed up into the saddle, her knees shook with the aftershock of almost unbearable tension. Until the moment that she'd buckled the halter over the massive neck, she hadn't really been sure that Pillar would tolerate it. 'I told you,' she grinned over at him, pretending nonchalance, 'Pillar's still just a baby at heart.' As she turned away, she blew a sigh of relief out through her cheeks, tugged gently on Pillar's halter rope, and started towards the edge of the plateau. The old bull followed obediently, and the cows followed him in a huddled mass. Cody brought up the rear, still shaking his head at what he had just witnessed, forgetting himself just long enough to let a smile touch his lips.

For the first hour of the long ride down, Tana was warmed by the glow of admiration she had seen in Cody's eyes, heard in his voice. She would never have had that from her father, or Zach, partly because neither of those men would ever have let her walk into the middle of the herd in the first place. Women didn't do such things out here. It just wasn't . . . fitting. It wasn't that her ability was questioned; it was just that men did certain things, and women did others, and that was all there was to that, and where would the world be if women started doing all the things men were supposed to do?

'It's hot, dirty, exhausting work,' Zach had told her once when she'd wanted to help with the spring branding. 'A job for men. Your job is being a woman. That's all you'll ever have to be.'

At the time she'd thought Zach was protecting her, but the more she thought about it, the more she wondered if perhaps he hadn't been protecting himself from the awful prospect of Tana learning she was capable of more than she knew.

But today a man had *expected* her to be capable, had expected her to do what she said she could do, and the experience had been intoxicating.

'He's really a remarkable man,' she told Clancey as the reliable horse picked his way carefully down a snowy slope. She leaned back in the saddle to balance her weight against the downward angle, then smiled suddenly, remembering something. 'And he's also a very good kisser.'

It was well after Tana's prediction of lunchtime as they crossed the last plateau before the final slope that led to the valley floor. Although the storm was increasing in intensity above them, there was little snow at this level; just a dusting across the grass. The cattle were dawdling now, heads bent to snatch a mouthful of dried grass.

Tana turned n the saddle, letting Clancey stop to graze as Cody cantered up behind her. He touched the brim of his hat as he reined Mac to a stop beside her, almost as if she were a lady he had just encountered on a city street.

'We're going to have our hands full now,' he told her, nodding towards the herd scattered behind them. 'Dumb as they are, these cows know there's a storm chasing them. The minute they see the ranch buildings, they're going to bolt for shelter. You ready for that?'

Tana pressed her lips together. How could she be ready for such a thing? Oh, she'd watched it often enough, but always from the safety of the fenced yard, eyes wide as she wondered how the cowhands managed to stay in the saddle as their horses darted and weaved beneath them.

Every autumn the herds came down from the summer pastures the same way—a bawling, thundering, confused mass of horns and hooves much too spread out to squeeze through the open gate of the huge paddock. As if by magic, the quick-turning cowponies always reformed the mass into a giant funnel and guided it unerringly through the gate, but it was frantic, dangerous work, and it wasn't unusual for an experienced cowhand to lose his seat in the confusion and find himself dodging sharp, panicked hooves on the ground. And, if an experienced hand could be caught off guard, what chance did she have?

'I'm ready,' she said, betrayed by the edge of fear in her voice.

When Cody didn't reply, she glanced over to find his eyes narrowed, as if he could actually see through her features to the scrambling, frightened thoughts beneath. 'You've never done anything like this in your life, have you?'

She shook her head wordlessly, and Cody sighed and looked away.

'Terrific. We'll probably both be trampled before this is over.' He lifted his hat and ran his hand back through his light hair, then replaced the stiff felt with the brim snug against his forehead. 'You'd better get that halter off the bull. The best we can hope for is that he'll be as anxious to get his herd home as we are.'

As Tana slid off Clancey's back to do his bidding, he continued a rapid-fire stream of instructions.

'You'll have to start down the slope in the lead, so the bull will follow, but as soon as they get going, you pull your horse out and to the side. Stay away from the herd, you understand?'

Tana climbed back into the saddle and nodded, brown eyes fixed attentively on Cody's blue ones as she nudged her toes barely into the stirrups, reciting her father's old warnings in her mind . . . 'Heels *down*, Tana. No! Not like that! Your foot's too deep in the stirrup! You won't be able to jerk it free if you fall, and that horse'll drag you to kingdom come!'

'. . . are you listening to me? You're going to

strangle that horse!' Cody's voice broke into her thoughts; sharp, and a little impatient. She looked down to where her hands had unconsciously tightened Clancey's rein, pulling the metal bit back against the corners of his mouth. She released the leather strips instantly to give the horse the slack he would need to manoeuvre.

'That's better,' Cody nodded. 'Now, as I said, you stay away from the herd. This is going to be the closest to a stampede you ever saw, so you let your horse take over. He'll know what to do. You just stay on him. I'll be pushing the cows from the back, trying to keep them together, but we might have some stragglers to round up down by the gate. You any good with that?'

Tana followed his gaze to the lariat coiled around her saddle horn, and shook her head.

'Great.' Cody stared off into the distance, his lips pressed into a hard line. 'Well, it's too late to give you a lesson now. You ready?'

'I'm ready,' she whispered.

'What?'

'I'm ready!' she shouted, controlling Clancey with her knees when he started at the sudden noise.

'Hey.' Cody reached over and grabbed her shoulder, frowning at the fear he saw in her face. Suddenly he arched one light brow and smiled at her, and once again the world went quiet for Tana. There was nothing in it now except for the easy, shining smile of this man; the confidence she saw in his eyes; the strength she felt in his hand. 'It's going to be all right,' he said softly, still smiling. 'These cows'll probably trot right into that paddock like a bunch of old ladies. But whatever happens, you'll be able to handle it. Trust me.'

Tana's eyes met his in a wash of liquid, golden brown and her lips curved upwards. 'I do,' she reminded him with all the earnestness of a bride's first vow.

Cody's brows twitched uncertainly and he jerked his hand away from her shoulder. 'Good,' he mumbled, settling himself into his saddle. The leather of his stirrups creaked with the downward pressure of his toes. 'Let's get started, then.'

She watched him as he turned Mac and jogged to the rear of the red and white living mass behind her. His hat barely moved against the darkening sky as he rode away, broad shoulders back, head high, hands and legs steady, Tana felt her heart lurch after him, almost as if it would follow on its own, leaving the shell of her body behind.

Finally he turned towards her, rose in the saddle, and waved her forward with the same gesture that had moved countless wagon trains across the plains over a century before. Tana responded to his signal as if it had been a push against her back, calling Pillar's name once, then urging Clancey over the lip of the plateau and down the slope towards the ranch.

For a few moments the herd followed placidly behind her, occasionally pausing to graze until Cody prodded them on with the familiar soft, staccato cry of the cowboy. Tana, tense with the anticipation of a sudden surge behind her, finally began to relax.

She saw the ranch spread out below like a child's collection of toys, placed in an orderly jumble against a painted backdrop of the most vivid scenery imaginable. A tiny, hustling ant-like figure scurried across the bare patch between house and barns as she watched, prompting a smile. Hazel must have been watching the trails non-stop to have seen them coming so quickly. Even now she was running to the paddock to open the huge gate. Thank heavens. At least that was one thing they wouldn't have to worry about.

Just as Tana twisted in the saddle to glance behind her, one cow in the herd, calling up a dim memory of last spring, apparently sensed shelter and food ahead and trumpeted a sound that sent shivers down Tana's spine and made Cody rise in his stirrups. Within the next second, four hundred and four split hooves dug sharply into the rocky slope and the living mass surged forward as a unit.

Shocked into helplessness at the speed with which the quiet ride had turned into a frantic gallop, Tana barely managed to keep her seat as Clancey bolted sideways, sped out of the way, then spun back to face the cattle. Rocking in the saddle at the sudden stop, Tana grasped her hat to her head as she watched the herd thunder down the slope before her eyes, picking up speed as it went.

'Come on!' she heard Cody's frantic call over the noise, and would have obeyed his command without question if her horse hadn't beaten her to it. With experience born of years of practice, Clancey was half sliding, half galloping down the steep slope, slowing at the bottom just long enough to assess the motions of the now panicked cattle, then driving forwards to close the ranks. All Tana could do was grip tight with her legs and give Clancey the rein he needed to do the job he knew so well.

At first the sudden stops and starts and turns of the horse between her legs terrified her. Although she had ridden almost every day of her life until she left the ranch for the city, she had never ridden a cowhorse while he was working. With each jolting motion, she became more and more certain that the next would certainly unseat her. And then, almost without realising it, she became so mesmerised by Clancey's instinctive skill that she relaxed, moving with the horse instead of against him, an admiring spectator in awe of the second sense of the creature that bore her.

With his head down, nose pointed to whatever cow dared to stray from the body of the herd, Clancey darted and veered, following every motion of the panicked target beast just ahead. He would balance on his hind legs more often than not, pivoting like a ballerina, almost as if he could sense the cow's next move before the cow decided on it. Without a single cue from Tana, Clancey dogged each stray mercilessly, forcing it back into the thundering herd, then spun to chase another with barely a wasted step.

For the first time in almost two days, Tana forgot her purpose, forgot the man who had consumed every waking thought since she had met him, and her heart soared with the exhilaration of the moment. At some point she had taken her cue from Clancey, whipped her hat from her head, and started leaning with the sharp turns, hooting at the strays, waving her hat to help the tireless horse bring the herd into the living funnel that was rapidly taking shape. Her hair flew behind in a dancing curtain of black as her slender body bent and rolled, one with the animal beneath her for the first time—not a woman on a horse, but a horse-woman, a single entity, performing a function it was born to.

As the first of the cows passed through the gate and into the paddock, Tana waved her hat madly at where Hazel stood behind the protection of the gate, mouth closed against the rising dust, eyes squinted nearly shut. But then Clancey sensed the milling discontent at the bottleneck, saw the panicked circling of the cows at the rear, and was off again, Tana moving with him, smiling fiercely in spite of the grit blown against her teeth.

Cody was matching her motions on the opposite side of the herd, trying to stretch and thin the funnel that fed through the gate, his head darting, his weight shifting automatically with the sudden moves of his horse, his concentration complete. The sight of man and horse performing so perfectly together left Tana breathless, and she watched in unabashed fascination, mindless of the spring-like leaps of the horse beneath her.

'Cody!' she cried in pure exhilaration, lifting her hat high, grinning until her cheeks hurt, wanting to reach across the dust-cluttered distance between them to give voice to the moment they were sharing.

Distracted, he jerked his head up and towards her, away from the motion of his horse, and Tana's grin vanished as she saw the panic in his glance. He hadn't heard the joy in her voice, only the cry he assumed meant trouble.

'No!' She started to holler that she was all right, but it was too late. He had tried to turn Mac into the herd, towards her, heedless of the danger, responding only to her call. Mac, thrown horribly off balance by the shift in weight and the sudden demand of the bit, lurched and then stumbled briefly to his knees, flinging his rider forward over his head, directly into the path of the last cows.

'No-o-o-o!' Tana screamed as she watched Cody fly from the saddle and then out of sight as the stampeding cows hid him with their bodies and hooves and dust.

Within a moment that stretched into a lifetime, Tana was on the ground, dodging the last of the cattle racing towards the gate, pounding through the dust that lay between her and the crumpled form on the ground.

She fell to her knees in the dust beside him, gasping for breath, her hands reaching tentatively for his shoulders. 'Cody?' Her panicked whisper was almost inaudible. 'Cody! Are you all right?' She had to close her eyes against the wave of sickness that rolled over her when he didn't respond. This was what happened when a stupid, greenhorn woman rode off in thoughtless bravado to do a man's work. It would have been all right if hers had been the only life she had risked; but the moment Cody agreed to ride with her, her inexperience had placed him in jeopardy too, and this was the result.

She stared down at the lifeless form, at the hunched back, the tucked legs, the quiet hands in a relaxed lace over the back of his head. He was dead. She'd slept in his arms last night, felt the astounding electricity of his mouth brushing hers, and now he was dead.

'No!' she screamed in unbridled fury against the enemy that had always lived in these mountains; the enemy that had taken her mother first, and then her father; the enemy she'd been running from for the past six years. A sudden flood of tears cut through the grime on her cheeks as she shouted at the still form, taking her anger out on him, since death was always so blithely unresponsive. 'Move, dammit!' she choked out, unwittingly slipping into the coarse vernacular of the range as anger blinded her thoughts. 'Move, you stupid, arrogant, cow-chasing bastard . . .'

She gasped, pulling words back into her throat as the still form groaned, then rolled slowly, painfully on to its side. 'All right, all right,' he moaned, spitting sand out of his mouth, easing full on to his back, blinking rapidly to clear his eyes. Squinting against the grit still lodged in the corners, he focused on her face, wiped one eye with the heel of his hand, then blinked again. 'You've got a hell of a bedside manner,' he said unevenly, blinking again, 'and a very interesting vocabulary for a history teacher.'

Tana's shoulders slumped as she released the breath she had been holding, and then her whole body crumpled like a boneless puppet's and she buried her head on his shoulder and cried.

Cody tried to lift a hand to comfort her, but it dropped back into the sand. 'Nice of you to worry about me,' he whispered into her hair.

She straightened and glared at him through her tears, inexplicably as furious now as she had been when she'd thought he was dead. 'What the hell did you think you were doing?' she shouted. 'Turning into the middle of a herd like that! Even *I* know better than that!'

'I thought you were in trouble,' he replied, his voice as dry as the dust he lay in, his mouth twisting in a half-smile. 'I was running to your rescue, in case you hadn't noticed.'

They both looked up at Hazel's wheezing, panting approach. 'Good lord! Good lord! How bad is it? Here,

Tana, out of the way, let me look.' She shouldered Tana aside and hunkered down beside Cody, her cheeks red with the cold, her dark eyes full of concern as they raced up and down his body, looking for injuries. Quick, gentle hands followed her gaze, and Cody winced when she felt his right ankle through his boot.

'Oh, hell.' His face screwed up with pain as he lifted himself slightly off the ground, reached for his leg, then fell back again, eyes closed, his features completely composed with the blessed relief of unconsciousness.

CHAPTER SIX

BY NIGHTFALL the storm had settled on to the massive ranch house, wrapping the weathered timbers in a swirling, white embrace. Pellets of icy snow drummed agains the windows, and curtains stirred against their rods as the wind gained entrance through invisible crevices.

Tana kept watch in the large second-storey bedroom that had been given over to Cody, her chair pulled close to the bed, her dark eyes intent on the form under the layers of quilts. She was warm and relaxed from a hot bath, bundled in a terry robe as white as the snow that now covered the yard. The unruly black mass of her hair, still damp from washing, was piled and clipped on top of her head, but a few curling tendrils escaped and lay coiled on the back of her neck and her forehead. Her blinks became slower, more languorous and, catching herself in a drowsy nod, she jerked back hard against the rungs of the chair to keep herself awake.

The room was dark, save for the glow of a single bedside lamp that sliced the sleeping man's face into stripes of light and shadow. He lay flat on his back, blond hair pushed away from his forehead, his chin lifted, as defiant in sleep as his hands had been, jerking the quilts down from his neck to expose one muscular shoulder and half of his bare chest. Tana had long since given up trying to keep him totally covered. Even unaware, he seemed to disdain the tender ministrations of women.

For reasons she didn't care to analyse, she couldn't make herself leave him to find her own rest, even though there was really no need to keep watch any longer. After five hours of wakening him regularly, the danger of concussion was past, and aside from a badly wrenched ankle his only other injuries were a collection of scrapes and bruises from the fall. Even that first, brief moment of unconsciousness had apparently been caused by the pain of his ankle, and he had wakened almost immediately. With Hazel's and Tana's support, he had been able to hop on one foot to the ranch house, up the stairs and into this very bed. It was only then that he had surrendered to exhausted sleep, barely stirring as they undressed him.

'Lord, you want to know if a man's a cowboy, strip him naked,' Hazel had remarked as they'd pulled off his dust-encrusted boots and jeans. 'Look at these legs. More scars than you can shake a stick at, and unless I miss my guess, this ankle's been broken once or twice. No wonder it sprained.'

Tana had examined the network of scar tissue across the long, muscular legs, recognising the telltale patterns of old wounds—a bull's horns had pierced there, just above the right knee, and the shin-bone beneath was pitted, marking many a fall from many a bronc. Hazel had pointed to a ragged circle of white scar-tissue on the discoloured swelling of his injured ankle, testament to where bone had once shattered and pierced the skin.

But what interested Tana more was the colour of the legs, and the rippling stomach, the arms and the chest. Even as something primitively familiar stirred within her at the sight of his naked body, she still noted the fading evidence of a summer tan, meeting a lighter line just above the waistband of his briefs, and that just didn't make sense. How would a cowboy get a tan? From leather chaps to long-sleeved shirt, each piece of the standard wardrobe was vital to protect against the thorny, lacerating bushes of the range. But if Cody's colouring could be believed, he'd spent the summer riding herd in swimming trunks, and brief ones at that.

Hazel either hadn't noticed the fading tan or hadn't thought to comment on it, so Tana had kept her silence as they soaked and wrapped the injured ankle and daubed antiseptic on the more serious scrapes.

But now, looking down on the golden skin stretched across his cheekbones, she wondered again at the oddity. He shifted his head slightly on the pillow, bringing the sharply defined line of his jaw fully into the light. She could see the pulse of life beating there, right where the jawbone made a sharp right angle up to the ear, and quelled an impulse to reach out and touch it.

She clasped her hands tightly in her lap and scowled, angry that she was finding these childish urges so hard to contain. He was just another cowboy—as arrogant and stubborn as the rest of them, cursed by pride to a pointless existence of constant struggle—precisely the kind of man and the kind of life she had run away from years before. Admittedly she had always been drawn to the sheer masculinity of such men, but maturity had granted her control over those responses; or so she had thought. Why should this man in particular shatter that control? Awaken feelings she had not felt since she was a teenager? Certainly Zach was every bit as handsome, in a dark, sinister way; and certainly he was every bit as self-assured and skilled in matters of the range—and yet, if Zach had been lying in this bed, would she be here now?

Suddenly she saw herself as she must appear, huddled by this bed as if her very life depended on every breath drawn by the man in it, a man she barely knew. Irritated by her own foolishness, she tensed her muscles to rise this instant and go to her own room and her well-deserved rest. But instead she pulled her chair even closer to the bed, crossed her arms on the quilt next to his body, and let her head sag down to rest there, just for a moment. Before the moment had passed, she was sound asleep, never noticing Cody's eyes opening to gaze at her quietly, never feeling the tentative touch of his fingers on one of the wayward coils of her damp hair.

Hours later, with the first light of dawn obscured by the raging blizzard outside, Hazel opened the door to Cody's room quietly, her dark brows lifting at the sight that met her.

Tana's head was pillowed on her arms on the brightly patterned quilt, one bare leg stretched outwards from the chair where her robe had slipped away. The cowboy's large, well-shaped hand rested on the back of her neck protectively, and a black curl was coiled around one of his fingers like the end of a leash. His face was turned towards Tana, as if he'd been watching her as he fell asleep.

Hazel took a step towards the bed with the thought of waking Tana before the cowboy saw her there, then looked at his hand on her neck again and realised he already had. She backed out of the room cautiously, grinning like an old fool, although she wasn't sure why, and closed the door softly behind her.

The first thing to penetrate Tana's awareness was a stiffness that started in her neck and stretched the length of her back; the second was a marked chill on her left leg; and the third was the unaccustomed weight of something resting on the back of her neck. She opened her eyes slowly, and when the pattern of the quilt shifted into focus, her heart thumped in alarm even as she forced herself to remain still. Much to her embarrassment, she realised she was still in Cody's bedroom, her head nestled in the curve of his waist, and from the quality of the light filtering through the drawn curtains it was past daybreak already. What would he think if he woke to find her here?

Slowly, slowly, a fraction of an inch at a time, wincing at the ache of muscles too-long confined in an awkward position, she eased her head to the side, away from the pressure of his hand, and then up off the bed. When she had finally completed the excruciatingly cautious movement, she shifted her gaze to his face and jumped when she saw his eyes fully opened, his mouth curved in amusement.

'Why didn't you tell me you were awake?' she snapped irritably, straightening in her chair, pulling the lapels of her robe more closely around her, avoiding his eyes.

'And a good morning to you, too,' he drawled, ending with a smiling yawn he covered with one hand.

Tana leaped to her feet, then collapsed on the bed as her left leg gave way beneath her. She tried to catch herself with her hands, but Cody snatched them away so she fell full-length next to him, and then wrapped his arms around her, chuckling, pulling her back up against his chest.

'I love an eager woman,' he murmured into her hair, trapping her arms just under her breasts as she began to flail and struggle, and this was how Hazel found them as she pushed the door open with a huge breakfast tray.

Tana's eyes flew wide and she stilled at the sight of Hazel's mischievous grin.

'I swear,' Hazel chuckled, approaching the bed, 'you two surprise me every single time I open that door. And from the progress you're making so far,' she nodded at Cody, 'I'm thinking I won't open it again without knocking first.'

'What could I do?' Cody grinned, opening his arms and letting Tana struggle up from the bed, her hair escaping its pins to spill over her shoulders, her face flushed with embarrassment. 'She just jumped in here with me before I could stop her.'

'Oh, be still!' Tana hissed over her shoulder, straightening her robe. 'My leg fell asleep and I fell on the bed, Hazel. That's all there was to it.'

Hazel nodded knowingly. 'Of course, child. I knew it was something like that.' She placed the tray on the bedside table and removed the piece of linen covering it, her little mouth curved in a knowing smile. Instantly the heady aroma of fresh-brewed coffee, hot cakes, bacon and eggs filled the room. She filled three cups and took one for herself over to a rocker in the corner. 'How's the ankle?' she asked Cody, watching his face tighten against the pain as he pushed himself to a sitting position.

Cody took a noisy sip from his cup, then glanced down at the lumps his feet raised under the quilt. 'What colour is it?'

'About as black as Tana's hair,' Hazel allowed with a nod, 'but it's not broken. I got a good feel of the bone before it swelled up too bad. It's a nasty sprain, though. You should stay off it for a few days.'

His face clouded for a moment, then he scooped a forkful of eggs into his mouth and mumbled around it, 'I'll have it looked at when I get into town.'

Tana, settled back into her chair with her own plate, glanced towards the window, then towards Hazel. The brown braid rocked with the sudden shake of the older woman's head. 'Hazel's tended more sprains and broken bones than just about any doctor in Montana,' she said, 'and it's a lucky thing she has. Take a look out of that window. You're not going anywhere, let alone the ninety miles to town.'

Cody stopped chewing, his eyes still on his plate. 'I came in a four-wheel drive,' he said without looking up. 'It'll get me back to town.'

'Not unless it sprouts wings,' Hazel chuckled from the corner. 'The Range Patrol called last night to say the road through the pass was already closed. Looks as if you're here to stay, cowboy.'

His plate tipped with the suddenness of his movement, and a piece of egg rolled on to the quilt. 'What are you talking about?'

Hazel's head rocked back on her shoulders at the sharpness in his tone.

'It's winter in Montana, son,' she said slowly, watching his face. 'Won't be anything but snow-mobiles moving in or out of this valley for some time to come. Any range-hand knows that . . .'

Somewhere in the back of Tana's mind, formless thoughts began to flutter like bats in a dark cave, searching for the way out. Cody spoke again before she could put it all together.

'I haven't ridden for the mountain ranches in a long time . . . guess I thought technology would have found a way around winter weather by now.' Meticulously, as if he were using the time to gather his own thoughts, he picked the stray piece of egg from the quilt and put it back on his plate. 'I'll need to make a call.'

'Phone went dead when I was talking to the Patrol.' Hazel shrugged. 'Lord knows when they'll get that working again. Lines could be down for weeks after a blizzard like this one.'

He muttered an expletive, then closed his eyes and leaned back against the headboard with a heavy sigh. 'Nothing ever changes out here, does it?' he asked no one in particular. 'All it takes is one little winter storm, and you're pioneers all over again, trapped in the last century. No phones, no way out, no power . . .' His eyes flew open and darted towards the bedside lamp, its glow still strong.

'Generator,' Hazel answered his unspoken question. 'I cranked it up when the power went last night, just after the phone.'

'Of course,' he nodded ruefully, as if he were recalling an old, old memory discarded years before.

'Come on, Tana.' Hazel rose briskly from her chair and moved towards the door. 'We'd better leave the man to his rest. And you,' she levelled a finger at Cody, 'you stay put until that ankle comes down to normal size again. You hear me?'

'Hazel,' Cody winced at the volume of her voice, 'they probably hear you in Idaho.'

CHAPTER SEVEN

'WHERE are you going?'

Tana looked up from pulling on heavy snow-boots as Cody stopped in the doorway of the large kitchen and braced himself with one hand against the wall.

She'd looked in on him a few times during the day, but he'd been buried under the covers of the old four-poster, as still and lifeless as a dormant seed waiting for spring. That motionless rise under the quilt hadn't prepared her for the power of his presence as he stood before her now.

His hair was slicked back off his brow, still wet from the shower, and his face was white with the strain of managing the stairs. He wore a short brown terry robe that sagged open at his chest, then dropped from a loosely belted waist to mid-thigh. His legs and feet were bare.

Tana caught herself staring at the slice of crisp blond curls exposed by the robe's parted lapels, then quickly turned her attention back to the intricacies of her boot-laces.

'It's a draughty house.' She spoke haltingly, like an uncertain schoolchild reading aloud for the first time. 'You'll freeze, dressed like that.'

'You're embarrassed.' She could hear the amusement in his voice and blushed, not daring to look up.

'I'm not used to men running around my house half-dressed. Of course it makes me uncomfortable.'

'Unless I miss my guess,' he drawled lazily, 'you've seen me in less. Or did Hazel take my clothes off and tend these scrapes all by herself?'

'That was different! You were asleep.'

'Oh, I see.' His voice was rich and mellow, coloured by a smile. 'Looking at naked men only bothers you when they're conscious . . .'

'Stop it!' She jerked her laces into a tight bow, slammed her boot on the floor and glared up at him.

'Sorry.' He shrugged with a disarming smile. 'It's just that you're an irresistible target for teasing. Besides, the truth is that this robe was the only thing hanging in the closet. I needed something to put on after a shower. My bag is still out in the jeep.'

Tana swallowed hard and reached for the white wool cap lying on the table. She jammed it on her head and started to tuck the thick mass of her hair up into it, using the process as an excuse not to look at him. 'I'll bring your bag in. I'm going out anyway.'

'Time to feed the cattle?'

Her nod loosened a strand of black from the cap and let it swing forward over her cheek. She tucked it back in, frowning. 'Twice a day, morning and evening, and it's almost sundown.' She looked up suddenly. 'Hazel's going to have your hide if she finds you out of bed, you know.'

He smiled a little when their eyes met, almost as if he were rewarding her for having the courage to look at him. 'I've been in bed all day. It's driving me crazy.'

She stood up and pulled a heavy wool parka from the back of the chair, then stopped in the motion of shrugging it on, mesmerised by his eyes. It was like looking at the sky in autumn, when the angle of the sun had lowered to reveal a deep, lustrous blue. The world was quiet then, catching its breath before the violence of coming winter, and that was what his eyes made her feel—as if something momentous, something heart-stopping and dangerous, was just around the corner. The feeling consumed her, tensed every muscle in her body, sent a rush of blood and adrenalin surging upward to colour her face and power her heart. 'It's good to see you up and about,' she said a little breathlessly. 'I'm glad you weren't badly hurt.'

His expression sobered abruptly, and a tiny muscle jumped in his jaw. 'The day may come when you wish otherwise.'

Tana frowned, uncertain how to respond to such a strange remark, and after a moment the quality of silence in the room and the intensity of his stare made her uncomfortable. She jumped when the ancient refrigerator kicked on with a noisy hum. 'Hazel's outside already,' she said, zipping up her coat hurriedly. 'I have to go.'

'I'll come with you . . .'

'Barefoot?' She nodded at his ankle, still an angry mix of black and blue, still too large to fit into any boot. 'We can manage. You get back to bed.'

She slipped through the door to the back cloakroom and closed it behind her, sagging against it and closing her eyes as if she'd just managed to escape something frightening. And then she heard what she was never intended to hear—the muffled sound of Cody's voice through the thick slab of wood, saying, 'Damn it. Damn it to hell.' She froze in place for a moment, her brows stitched in puzzlement. Part of her wondered why he sounded so desperately, helplessly bitter; and part of her didn't want to know. Quickly, quietly, she slipped through the outside door.

For some reason she felt safer in the frigid open spaces of the snowswept yard, or at least distracted from her own thoughts by nature's demonstration of chilly power. The freshening wind scoured her face like sandpaper, and miniature tornadoes of snow danced and swirled from the heels of her lifted boots. She put her head down and strode briskly towards the loafing shed on the far side of the yard, just barely visible through the driving snow. We'll have to string a guide line from the house tomorrow if it gets much worse, she thought, squinting so her lashes would deflect the driving pellets. Just as they did in pioneer days. Cody was right about that. Winter knocks this part of the country back a full century.

The loafing shed was an enormous rectangular building, its back nestled against a slope, huge sliding doors on its front opening into the paddocks. Tana followed Hazel's rapidly fading tracks to a side door that opened on to a tractor drive-through, slipped inside, and closed the door behind her with relief. It was still bitterly cold, but it was better inside, away from the wind that sapped body heat in a matter of seconds.

A wall on her left separated the drive-through from the open arena that took up almost the entire ground floor of the building. When she and Hazel had driven them inside earlier in the afternoon, Pillar and the cows had looked lost in the space designed to shelter more than three hundred cows from winter storms; but they'd seemed happy enough when the sliding door had closed behind them, locking the storm outside.

To Tana's right a ladder led to a first-storey loft that was packed with the sweet-smelling bales of summer hay. Agile in spite of her bulky clothes, she climbed quickly and joined Hazel in the loft.

They worked in silence while the wind battered the thin aluminium skin of the shed and the cold seeped in through every crevice. Within moments their condensed breath had frozen into a frost that whitened their lashes and brows and stiffened the scarves wrapped around their faces. Panting with exertion, they curled their mittens around the twine of bales, then dragged them to trap-doors in the floor so they could be pushed through to the milling cattle below.

Shivering in spite of her many layers of clothing, Hazel grunted as she pushed a particularly heavy bale across the floor towards a trap door. 'If you ask me,' she grumbled, 'we should kill every one of these damn beasts and eat them.'

Tana smiled behind her scarf, throwing her own weight behind the bale. 'You think this is bad? Wait until the storm lets up and we have to carry hay out to the paddocks.'

Hazel fell forward on to her hands, her shoulder heaving, as the hay finally slipped through the opening.f 'By that time Cody will be better,' she panted, 'and I'll be snug in my kitchen while you two kill yourselves out here.'

'Cody wants to leave,' Tana reminded her.

'Doesn't matter what Cody wants. The man can't get out until the pass opens . . .' she leaned back on her heels and cocked her head, her eyes sparkling as a thought struck her '. . . and come to think of it, Zachary can't get in. Well, now, how about that? This blizzard's beginning to look more and more like a godsend every minute.'

Tana rested on her knees, her hands jamming against her hips in exasperation. 'Hazel, you don't make any sense. Zach's been proving himself around here for nine years. We don't know Cody at all. How can you favour a complete stranger?'

Hazel cocked her head and stared at her for a moment. 'I'm not the only one who favours him,' she said pointedly, nodding when Tana lowered her eyes. 'Besides, Cody belongs here. I knew that the minute I laid eyes on him.'

Tana sighed and struggled to her feet, knowing it was hopeless to argue, and not sure she wanted to anyway. 'Come on, you old mystic. We've got another thirty bales to move, and if I get any hungrier, I might start eating some of this stuff myself.'

It was over an hour later when the women finally fought the wind-driven snow across the yard, then stomped into the back cloakroom to leave their outer garments to thaw over the floor-drain. Exhausted, cheeks bright red from the cold, they pushed through the door to the kitchen and stopped dead, numbed lips parted in amazement.

'Good lord,' Hazel found her voice first, 'would you look at this?'

The large wooden table was set for three, a bowl of tossed green salad in its centre, and the aroma of baking savoury biscuits filled the room. Cody straightened from peering through the glass in the oven door and brushed his hands on the front of his robe, leaving white, floury streaks on the brown terry cloth.

'About fifteen more minutes,' he said, reaching for two already filled glasses and handing them to the flabbergasted women. 'Time for one cocktail.'

'You made supper,' Tana murmured in disbelief.

'Not at all. Hazel's had that stew going all day. I just threw together a few things to go with it.' He cocked his head and frowned at their identical expressions. 'Well? What's the matter with you two? Hasn't a man ever cooked in this kitchen before?'

They both shook their heads simultaneously, mouths still open, and Cody smiled in amusement. 'It's a brand new world, ladies. These days men cook, they clean, some of them even take care of their own children. It's the twentieth century, you know.'

'Not out here, it isn't,' Hazel said, dropping into a chair at the table, staring at the drink in her glass as if she'd never seen one before.

Cody slid his own drink from the counter, glanced over at Tana, and lifted his glass in a private, silent toast. His eyes never left hers as he drank.

Wordlessly, almost mindlessly, she followed his motions like a mirror reflection, lifting her glass to her lips, drinking, staring at him over the rim. The heat of the drink coursed down her throat, and there was something almost erotic about the sensation, simply because he was witnessing it. She thought she saw his eyes narrow slightly as he watched, but he turned away before she could be sure.

'How bad is it out there?' he asked with feigned lightness, apparently intent on whatever was happening in the stew pot on the stove.

'Bad enough,' Hazel answered him. 'The drive's under a couple feet of snow already, and the wind's packing it like cement. You're here for a while, cowboy, if that's what you're wondering.'

Cody's brows and lips came together in a frown as he replaced the cover on the stew. 'In that case,' he said with a strange tightness Tana hadn't heard in his voice before, 'there are a few things you two had better know about me.'

'What's to know?' Hazel chuckled, slurping noisily from a glass that was rapidly emptying. 'You've got a strong back and an easy manner and you're good to look at. Don't need to know any more than that to winter with a man.'

'Hazel!' Tana gasped.

'Well, it's the truth, isn't it? There's fate at work here. Cody was meant to stay.'

Cody's attempt at a smile was troubled. 'Fate?'

'No doubt about it,' Hazel nodded emphatically. 'What else would you call it? The future was blacker than pitch a couple days ago—no money, no cattle, no way to stop D.C. from taking away the ranch—then the minute you showed up, Cody, things started to come around. Even the weather is on our side—it's keeping D.C. out, and you in. I'm telling you, it's fate.'

'Hazel, you drank that too fast,' Tana scolded her, turning to share a smile with Cody, frowning when she saw that he was ignoring both of them, stirring the stew furiously.

'Sit down,' he said gruffly, snatching hot biscuits from the tin and dropping them on to a platter. 'Everything's ready.'

Hazel and Tana exchanged puzzled glances at the sudden shift to curtness in his tone, then shrugged puzzlement away in the novelty of being served by a man for the very first time.

'Can you see Zach doing this?' Hazel grinned, breaking apart a hot biscuit, watching the steam escape.

'Who's Zach?'

'Foreman,' she mumbled through a mouthful, her eyes on Cody as he limped to the table with a cauldron of stew and then eased gingerly into his chair. 'Off tending his sick brother now, thank heavens. First peace I've had in this house in nine years.'

Tana raised her brows at the pleasant tang of some unidentified spice in the salad dressing, then remembered to scowl at Hazel. 'Don't pay any attention to her,' she told Cody. 'Zach's been our foreman for over nine years now, and you couldn't find a better man. He managed on his own when Dad was laid up, even after the rest of the hands left. He and Hazel just never got along.'

'Then there must be something wrong with him,' Cody said, planting a broad smile on the older woman's face.

Tana tossed her hair over her shoulders. 'Or something wrong with Hazel's judgement. No one could have done more than Zachary to keep this ranch going, and as far as I can tell from the books, he's worked almost a full year without a dime in pay. I think he felt worse than either of us when everything fell apart.'

'Oh, I don't know,' Hazel said slowly. 'Seems to me things are looking pretty good for old Zach right about now. He's still got land of his own, and he was about to get the grandaddy of all prizes, now wasn't he?'

There was an awkward silence at the table. Cody's fork stopped half-way to his mouth as his eyes darted back and forth between the two women. 'What prize?'

'That one.' Hazel nodded at Tana.

Cody's head turned slowly. 'You?'

'He offered to marry me, that's all,' she said quickly, looking down at her plate. 'To make a place for all of us on his new ranch, because we were losing this one.'

Cody leaned back in his chair slowly, still staring at her downcast eyes. 'Offered, did he?' he said quietly, somehow making Zach's proposal sound like an insult. 'And what did you say?'

'I told him I needed time to think,' she mumbled, jamming a forkful of salad into her mouth so she wouldn't have to answer any more questions. She chewed self-consciously, staring straight ahead, her face colouring just because she felt his eyes on her.

CHAPTER EIGHT

TANA stretched full-length on the living-room couch, her arms behind her head, her face turned towards the fireplace, blissfully limp with relaxation. For some reason, today's relatively easy schedule had been more exhausting, more fraught with tension than yesterday's mad dash down the slope towards the paddocks. Probably because Cody had been so strange today, so different from when they'd been alone, up on the mountain. In spite of the cold and the danger up there, he'd been much more at ease—in his element, of course. Maybe it was the confines of the house that irritated him, as it would irritate any ranch-hand used to life in the open. Still, the tension that crackled through him at supper was almost palpable, and definitely contagious. She was relieved to go upstairs for her shower after the dishes; even more relieved to find the downstairs deserted afterwards. Apparently Cody and Hazel had both gone to bed early, and Tana was savouring her solitude.

She stretched her legs until her bare toes peeped out from beneath the hem of her old powder-blue dressing-gown. She'd smiled to see it hanging on the bathroom door when she'd gone in to shower, and although she knew Hazel must have just resurrected it from storage it seemed as though it had been hanging there for the past six years, just waiting for her to come back. There was something about the way the soft, worn flannel draped easily over her body, something about the way it swished against her legs when she walked, and that something felt right; it felt like home.

She fingered the knot of thread at the collar where a button had been missing as long as she could remember, thinking that the human animal was a strange creature indeed, to find security in something as simple as a few yards of old cloth.

She jumped a little as a ball of pine sap exploded in the fire, then let herself go limp again. Funny. She'd expected to feel horribly alone sitting in front of the fireplace where she and her father had spent so many of the evenings of her youth, but instead she had found a strange sort of comfort here, as if the fireplace, like her dressing-gown, had been waiting all these years for her return. The sense of homecoming was so strong that she'd even smiled a little as she dried her long hair in front of the flames, and by the time she crawled up on to the couch she was beginning to believe that this land, this house, might be where she belonged, after all. Could that really be? Was it possible that she had actually run in a six-year circle that had brought her right back to where she started?

She rolled on her side and focused on the magnified strands of her hair, lying in a glossy black sheet over her arm.

I'll cut it tomorrow, she thought drowsily, snuggling deeper into the worn leather cushions, pushing a stray strand away from eyes she could barely manage to keep open. A ranch-hand has no business with hair this long, and that's what I am now, isn't it—a ranch-hand? No use even trying to pretend I'll go back to teaching, back to the city, back to tailored suits and high heels. Not after yesterday.

Finally she let her eyes close and listened to the quiet symphony of the fire and the distant, muted howl of the wind embracing the house.

She didn't know how long she'd been asleep, or even if she'd been asleep, when some sixth sense made her roll on to her back and open her eyes. She gasped when she saw Cody standing behind the couch, looking quietly down at her.

'Sorry.' His lips twitched in what might have been the beginning of an apologetic smile, but his eyes never wavered from hers. 'I didn't know anyone was in here. I thought you'd gone to bed.'

She jerked to a sitting position and scooted into the corner of the couch, her bare feet tucked under her. 'I thought *you'd* gone to bed. How long have you been standing there?'

'Not long.' His eyes dropped to her neck, seemed to focus on where the missing button of her gown should be, then he turned and limped across the room to the window and peered out into the snowy night.

Tana watched him walk away, oddly graceful in spite of the limp, and fought the same surging breathlessness that used to assault her when she watched Zach ride away on his horse, back when she was a teenager.

But you're not a teenager any more, she reminded herself angrily. You're too old to be feeling what you're feeling, just because a cowboy walks into the room. Besides, he doesn't even look like a cowboy now . . .

And he didn't. Her eyes narrowed at the elegance of his figure as it was framed by the blackened glass, and suddenly she realised that the trappings of ranch-hand were gone. No boots, no hat, no chaps—he could have been any man, in any house, in any city in the world— and still her heart fluttered in her breast and she had to concentrate to breathe normally. She watched him lift one hand and run it back through his hair, watched the strands of multicoloured blond shift and fall into layered perfection beneath his fingers, and suddenly it seemed as if his hand were threading through *her* hair, not his, catching in a tangle, pulling her head back, exposing her neck . . .

She dropped her chin abruptly, blinking hard against the power of her own imagination. '*That's* the change of clothes you had in your bag?' she asked quickly, noticing for the first time what precisely he was wearing.

He glanced down at his shirt, then back over his shoulder at her. She felt the impact of his eyes across the room. 'This is it. Why?'

Had he asked her a question? Of course he had, but what was it? It was impossible to concentrate when he looked at her like that, as if his gaze alone had the power of touch, the magic ability to reach across a room and smoke against her cheek, and down her neck . . .

Damn. What was the question?

'Something wrong with what I'm wearing?' he asked quietly, and she knew from the thickness of his voice that the question had been automatic; that he cared no more for the answer than she did.

'Silk shirts and dress trousers aren't exactly the standard cowboy uniform,' she murmured.

A light, fluffy sweep of hair angled across his forehead and bounced a little as he walked towards her, but she saw this only peripherally. Her attention was focused on his eyes. Her own felt huge, liquid, growing larger with every step he took, capable of swallowing him whole if he only got close enough.

'I was supposed to be in the city by this time,' he said, stopping less than a foot from the arm of the couch her hands clutched with a white-knuckled grip. 'Chaps and boots are as out of place there as this get-up is here. Mind if I sit down?'

She shook her head slowly, closing her eyes when his weight shifted the cushion beneath her, feeling as if she'd been touched. She risked a sideways glance at his knees, saw the sharp crease of his trousers pointing towards the fire, then falling away into nothingness.

'Give that ankle a rest. Put your leg up on the couch.'

He released a pained sigh and let his head fall back, turned so he could look at her. 'This is fine,' he said, but he was rubbing hard at the thigh of his injured leg.

'Did you take some aspirin?'

'I don't need it.'

It was a tremendous relief to jump from the couch, to stomp out of the room and away from his eyes, if only for a moment. Her bare feet slapped against the floorboards when she returned with aspirin in one hand and a glass of water in the other. 'Here. Stop being so damn stoic and take these.' She shoved her hand at him.

'Yes, ma'am,' he grinned, fingering the tablets in her palm, but then she trembled at his touch and hitched in a tiny, startled breath, and his fingers stilled in her hand and his grin faded as he looked up at her, the blue of his eyes dark and shuttered.

'Take them!' she said, almost desperately, dumping the pills when he opened his hand, spinning away abruptly. Her hands fumbled at her sides, looking for something to do, and then she bent and bodily lifted his injured leg to the couch. 'Now, leave it there,' she commanded, turning her back to look at the fire. 'What city were you going to?'

'Dallas.'

She felt his voice ripple up her spine and pressed her lips together in frustration. Even having her back turned was no protection.

'Dallas?' She turned back to the couch, purposefully sat with her body angled towards him, her right arm draped across the back, as if she were perfectly comfortable, perfectly at ease. 'Why Dallas?'

'I have some business interests there,' he said in a dull, hypnotic monotone while his eyes swept over her face, lingering at her lips, dropping to where the white skin of her neck disappeared beneath the powder-blue of her gown. She forgot to breathe as she watched the journey of his gaze, her own eyes wide and unblinking. The soft, full mound of her breast rose beneath her gown when his eyes touched it, and she heard him respond with a quick intake of breath. His eyes narrowed to slits of blue flame as the cords of his neck sprang suddenly into relief, and Tana felt her own nostrils flare with forgotten breath, felt the heavy thump of a heart finally remembering to beat, and in some distant corner of her mind she realised that he was making love to her with his eyes.

'Cody . . .?' She'd said it so softly, so tentatively, but the word exploded like a gunshot on his face. His head jerked back on his shoulders, the blue fire in his eyes darkened, smouldered, then died, and his lips jerked in the afterthought of a cold smile. Tana felt as if a window had suddenly opened somewhere, sucking all the heat out of the house. 'It's getting colder, isn't it?' she said lamely, getting up to put another log on the fire, huddling on the hearth for a moment, thoroughly confused, before returning to her seat on the couch.

Instead of answering her question, he looked directly at her and asked one of his own; something totally unrelated. 'You've decided to make a go of it, haven't you?'

She hesitated, her dark brows reaching for one another over her nose. 'What?'

'You've decided to stay. To work the ranch yourself.'

'I . . . I was thinking about that very thing before you came in.'

'And?' His voice dug into her mind, prodding for confirmation she hadn't even acknowledged to herself yet.

She looked down at her hands, twisting together in her lap. Why was he pushing? Why was there such insistence behind his words, such a demand to know? Yes, she'd decided she couldn't go back to the city, but that was as far as her thoughts had taken her. They hadn't yet travelled down that troubled, pitted road that led to becoming a real rancher. She didn't have to make that decision just yet, did she? There were still other alternatives . . . like Zach . . .

Her expression cleared suddenly as the real options loomed before her. She had two choices. She could become a rancher, or she could become a rancher's wife—specifically, Zach's wife. 'Yes,' she said calmly. 'I've decided. This is the Mitchell Ranch, and I'm a Mitchell.'

He nodded once, then turned his head and stared at the fire. 'Rumour had it that Everett Mitchell's daughter hated ranching. That she'd never want to stay on after her father died.'

Tana looked down at where she was fingering a fold in her gown and spoke softly. 'The rumours were true. But somehow things have changed. I'm not sure even I understand it yet.'

'But you're staying.'

'Yes.'

She couldn't read his eyes, any more than she could have read the meaning behind the nuances of colour in a summer sky, but she thought she detected a trace of bitterness behind his smile; a trace of irony.

'It's the land, isn't it?' he murmured at the fire, almost as if he were talking to himself. 'Something about the land . . . no matter how far you go, or how long you manage to stay away, in the end, it always calls you back.' He closed his eyes briefly, then turned to look at her. 'Hellfire,' he whispered, barely moving his lips. 'A man could drown in your eyes.'

Almost in slow motion, Tana's lips parted, her eyes widened, and her hand rose until her fingers rested on the pulse in her throat.

Suddenly he jerked his head away, shaking it as if he were angry with himself. 'And that's just about enough of that, isn't it?' He dropped his foot to the floor and stood up quickly. 'Time I was going to bed. Past time, as a matter of fact.'

Tana sat there for a long time after he'd left the room, staring into the fire, wondering if her heart would ever slow down.

CHAPTER NINE

THE DAYS quickly settled into a routine Tana remembered from all the snowbound winters of her youth—short showers, no television, a favouring of darkened rooms to bright lights—everything done with a mind to saving the huge basement generators for what was most important—keeping the electric heaters in the cattle water tanks going full blast, and providing enough electricity to run the fan on the oil-burning furnace. Within the space of a single winter storm, the Mitchell Ranch had slipped back over a hundred years.

Contrary to the misconceptions of her city acquaintances, there were still places in the mountainous regions of the American West that were immutably ruled by the whims of winter. On those valley ranches accessed by a single road winding through a mountain pass, the door to twentieth-century civilisation slammed abruptly closed with the first blizzard, and sometimes didn't open again until spring.

Nestled in the moist cradle of the Big Snowy Mountains, winter isolation was a fact of life on the Mitchell Ranch, and the routine was the key to survival. The autumn preparation of gasoline generators to provide power, the careful storage of fresh produce and vegetables in the root cellars, the meticulous stocking of pantries that held enough food to last a winter through—all of these things were a matter of course to those isolated pockets of humanity who chose the wilderness for their home.

Tana barely noticed when she stopped resenting the hardships and began to take pride in her ability to survive them. But Cody did.

'You're actually enjoying this, aren't you?'

It was a full week after his accident, three days since he'd taken Hazel's place helping with the chores. They were up in the loft shoving hay bales through the trap doors to the cattle waiting below. They were almost finished with the evening feeding, and Tana was exhausted and bone-cold. Strands of black were plastered to her perspiring brow beneath her wool cap, and frozen puffs of breath escaped her mouth with the hoarse regularity of a steam engine just coming up to speed.

She dropped back on her heels and stared at him, astounded by the question. 'You've got to be kidding,' she gasped. 'There isn't a single muscle in my body that isn't screaming right now, my nose is so cold it feels like it's going to fall off, and you think I'm having a good time?'

He grinned and gestured with his frosted mitten. 'But you're smiling. All the time, you're smiling.'

Her mouth formed an amazed circle. 'I am?'

He shook his head, chuckled, and went back to work while she remained kneeling, watching his arms swing a bale that weighed more than she did over to the trap door. He flipped the bale, peeling the twine away that had held it together, then tipped his head sideways to look at her. He'd pushed the hood of his parka back on to his shoulders long ago, and strands of dark blond, sweat-dampened hair stuck to his forehead in spite of the cold. 'Who elected you foreman?' he teased her, and because he was usually so serious she reacted to the light-heartedness of his tone with a broad smile.

'See what I mean? Smiling, all the time smiling.'

Was she? She felt the dry coldness of cheeks her mouth was lifting, and conceded that she was, and when she thought about it, it was pretty remarkable. She'd spent six years of her life either absorbing or dispensing higher education, and not one of the moments in all of those years elicited the satisfaction she felt in the dumb physical labour of tossing these hay bales around. Her city friends would be horrified.

Part of the pleasure came from having Cody at her side, of course; not simply because he was superficially attractive, not even because he exuded the cowboy's aura of masculinity in waves that almost overpowered her at times, but because she felt a deeper bond with him than she had felt with any other human being, a subconscious sense that he was rediscovering the purity of ranch life right along with her, as if he, too, had almost lost it forever.

But whenever she acted on that sense of closeness, probing with a question, an intrusive glance, or even an inadvertent touch, he backed off immediately, slamming an interior door against her. That one electric night by the fire, a night that should have opened communication between them, had strangely had the opposite effect. By his design, she was sure, they had not been alone together since, except when they did chores.

And that didn't count, she thought glumly, rising to her feet, reaching for another bale. Breath was too precious to waste on idle conversation when they were working, and Cody always set the pace back to the house when they were finished. It was not only brisk, it was very nearly marathon calibre.

'Five more bales,' Cody sang out.

Unconsciously, Tana slowed her pace, dragging a bale across the loft floor as if her arms were too weak to lift it. When they finished the chores, they would go back to the house, back to Hazel, and she wouldn't be alone with him any more. He'd see to that, although she didn't quite understand why. He'd been just as moved as she had that night by the fire, hadn't he? So why was he avoiding her? Why did he rush to bed so quickly on the heels of Hazel that it was almost comical? Why did he always take a chair as far from her as possible when the three of them sat by the fire in the evenings? Why did he only watch her surreptitiously, jerking his eyes away the moment she looked up?

'You're avoiding me.' She was standing up straight, hands on hips, glaring at him, and the accusation was out of her mouth before she realised she was going to speak at all.

He was hunched over a bale, his back towards her, and his hands stopped in the motion of twisting off the twine. After a long moment he straightened to his full height—slowly—and turned to face her.

For just one instant, when he was still partially in profile, Tana thought she detected a troubled frown; but by the time he'd turned fully around his brow was clear, the blue eyes beneath deceptively innocent.

'Now, where did you get such an idea?' he asked. 'We're together almost every waking minute, either in the house, or out here.'

'But not alone. You're afraid to be alone with me. You have been, ever since that night by the fire.'

There was an instant of hesitation before his comeback. 'I don't know what you're talking about. We're alone right now.'

'You know what I mean.'

He closed his eyes, raised his brows, and let a frosty plume of air escape his pursed lips. He looked off to the side when he finally spoke in slow, measured tones. 'Let's just say I'm no saint, Tana.'

She cocked her head. 'Meaning?'

He turned and looked straight at her. 'You know damn well what I mean.'

She stood perfectly still, her eyes luminous in the dim light of the loft. Finally he had to turn away from her gaze.

'Letting something happen between us wouldn't be fair to you,' he grumbled. 'You expect too much. Things that aren't there, some . . . deeper connection between us, and the simple truth is that we're just a man and a woman, thrown together, responding to the same biological attraction that would happen between *any* man and woman under the same circumstances.'

At first the cold, impersonal assessment hit Tana like a fist in the stomach, but then she realised that she hadn't said a single thing about some deeper connection between them. He'd said it first. Her eyes widened slightly as this new knowledge tugged her lips into a wondering smile. 'You feel it, too, don't you?' she whispered.

His head jerked at that and his eyes narrowed suspiciously. 'Feel what?'

She shrugged helplessly. 'Whatever it is you claim isn't there.' Without fully realising what she was doing, she moved to within a foot of him and looked up, her brows tipped, her lips parted in an unconscious invitation. 'We're alike, you know . . .'

'Alike?' he shouted, stumbling backwards as if she'd attacked him. 'Of course we're alike! That's the problem! We're so much alike, you wouldn't believe it!'

She hesitated, frowning, her hand frozen in the gesture of reaching for him. 'I don't understand.'

'You will,' he replied in a flat voice, his expression suddenly, eloquently miserable. 'Some day.' He turned away from her and went back to his work.

It was a bleak, foreboding prophecy, and it kept Tana sullen and silent through the rest of the evening chores. They'd just finished filling the water tanks and were ready to leave the shed for the house when Cody stopped her with a hand on her arm. 'Look at him,' he said, nodding towards Pillar. The old bull stood over the tank, massive head lifted, water dripping from his muzzle as he contemplated them with a liquid gaze that almost seemed intelligent. 'He's a magnificent bull,' Cody murmured absently. 'I've never seen better. You could build an empire on stock like that.

'We did,' she replied, following his gaze. 'And I'll do it again.'

He turned his head to look at her then, and for once his expression was unguarded. 'Don't you think you should find out how you lost the first one before you start building on a second?'

She felt herself begin to melt under the directness of his gaze, had to look away before she could respond, and even then, her words sounded distant, as if someone else had said them. 'I already told you. Drought, disease, debts . . . it happens out here.'

Cody looked back at the bull. 'Maybe. Still, you should make sure.'

Tana sighed, too absorbed in the way his face looked in profile to concentrate seriously on anything else. 'It's history,' her voice said, although she couldn't remember commanding the words. She watched the curve of his lashes when he blinked, memorised the line of his jaw, and wondered why his confirmation that they were alike had sounded like a death sentence. Being alike, things in common, shared thoughts and dreams ... that was what brought people closer together, wasn't it? She had to force herself back to the subject of the conversation. 'What made the ranch fail doesn't matter any more, anyway. What matters now is getting it going again, and thanks to Pillar and these cows I can do that.' She hesitated, then looked up at him with a bright smile. 'And thanks to you, of course. I couldn't have done it without you, Cody ... what's so funny? Why are you laughing?'

He never told her.

They were all lingering over after-dinner coffee, Hazel leaning back in her chair with her hands laced across her stomach, Cody hunched over his cup, staring into it, and Tana with one elbow propped on the table, her chin in her hand. She was staring at Cody, just as she had through the whole meal, and she was enjoying the fact that it obviously made him nervous.

She couldn't control the affinity she felt for him, a spiritual closeness that had seemed to increase day by day; and, even though he'd refused to acknowledge that out in the shed, at least he'd admitted to a physical attraction. At least he couldn't ignore her completely.

What dark, terrible secret kept him so distant, so removed? Now that she thought about it, he'd been dancing around direct questions about his life for days, laughingly refusing to talk about himself or his past, always shifting the conversation so skilfully that not even Hazel suspected he was hiding something. Was he a criminal on the run? A wayward husband seeking escape from the ties of marital responsibility? Or was he just what he appeared to be: an itinerant cowboy hopping from place to place, close-mouthed as they all were, leery of emotional attachments that would ultimately threaten his freedom? Could it really be that simple?

She'd decided days ago that it didn't matter who Douglas Cody had been, only who he was now, and the man he was now had a taste for these mountains and valleys, an appetite for this life, that reminded her of those fleeting years of utter freedom she'd felt on this ranch as a young girl. It hadn't seemed like freedom then, of course—not to a teenage girl who dreamed of brights lights and theatres and restaurants and all the other lures of the city. But now, having seen the shabbiness behind the lights, the hive-like mentality of the denizens of man-made mountains of steel and glass, she felt like a wild creature confined for years in a zoo, just recently released to experience a freedom she had almost forgotten. Articulating such a feeling would have been impossible, but with Cody she didn't feel she had to. It was almost as if they were rediscovering common memories together, sharing them in quiet, inarticulate ways that were felt more than heard or seen. Like the night she'd found him outside in the front yard, his head tipped back, staring up at the immense inverted bowl of star-spangled Montana sky. It had been three days after the storm, and a bitter wind still swept the range, crusting the snow into impassable drifts that mimicked the mountains, but the clouds had moved eastward, and the sky was clear.

He'd glanced down at her approach, then lifted his head again, and there was something noble about his stance; something almost unspeakably proud. Tana knew how humbling the majestic immensity of a Montana night sky could be to all except those few who belonged under it; the men and women who took their living from the land with grateful, nurturing reverence. These were the people who had earned the right to stand beneath this sky with their heads up and their shoulders back. Her father had been one, and Douglas Cody was another. Hazel was right. He belonged here. He'd startled her then, by putting her own thoughts into words that applied to her, not him. 'You belong here,' he'd told her without looking down, and the clarity of that simple truth was so suddenly obvious that she couldn't for the life of her understand why she had ever tried to deny it.

She was remembering that night as she stared at Cody now, and she didn't see a tired man listening intently to Hazel's ramblings, blond hair tumbling over his brow—she saw the man outside, head lifted, shoulders back, eyes taking in the wonder of a night sky with the possessiveness of a lover.

'. . . and that's when things really started to go downhill,' Hazel was saying, apparently in response to a question about the ranch finances. 'And if the late spring blizzard wasn't enough, then we had drought to contend with. Worst one I can remember, and I've been around a few years, I can tell you.' She shook her big head and her face screwed up in a fierce frown. 'The grazing was so poor that Zach had to spend a fortune on supplemental feed, but even that didn't help. By that time the cattle's resistance was too low. Disease started striking them down by the hundreds. Ah!' She brushed at her eyes with her fists and shook her shoulders. 'No point going over this again. No point at all. They were bad, bad times.'

Tana reached over and touched Hazel's arm. 'But they're over,' she reminded her with a gentle smile. 'Come spring, we'll sell the calves those cows are carrying, and we'll have enough to pay off the contract on this place and start again. It's going to be all right, Hazel.'

Hazel glanced up at the child she had comforted and nurtured for years, and experienced that sudden, painful wrenching a parent feels when it finally becomes apparent that the tables have turned, that the child is now an adult, assuming the caring role. 'I know that, Tana,' she said a little sadly. 'I knew that the minute you decided to stay. As long as there's just one Mitchell on this ranch, we'll keep the wolves from the door.' Her gaze moved to encompass Cody. 'And with Douglas here too, we're downright invincible.'

Cody shifted awkwardly in his chair, cleared his throat, then started stacking dishes noisily to carry to the sink.

'Oh, stop.' Hazel shooed him from the room with a flick of her apron, and included Tana in the dismissal with a stern look. 'You two get the living-room fire laid while I clean up in here, then we'll all sit around and drink brandy, just like the city folks.'

'Brandy?' Cody's brows shot up. 'You've got brandy?'

'For special occasions,' Hazel said sternly, then her

face softened. 'And special friends. Go on, now.'

Tana sat on the couch, legs crossed, and watched Cody crouch at the hearth, laying a pyramid of wood as ancient in design as mankind itself. 'You want to know if a man's a cowboy, ask him to build a fire,' she said suddenly, smiling at the shredded kindling heaped in the empty space at the pyramid's base, structured to shelter the infant flames from the fickle range wind. 'That's what my father always said.'

'Is that how your dad started out? As a cowboy?' He struck a huge wooden match on the hearth and touched it to the shavings.

'Before I was born,' Tana mused, staring into the flames. 'Only he was a little different from most of the men he rode with.'

Cody prodded at her memory like he prodded at the fire. 'In what way?'

'He had a dream,' Tana sighed. 'A big dream, for a cowboy. He wanted a place of his own. So he skimped and saved and went without, and after he married my mother he worked the rodeo circuit as a bronc buster for extra cash, and finally, by the time I was eight years old, he had enough for a down-payment on this place.'

Cody was balanced in a crouch on the balls of his feet, his arms draped across his knees as he stared at the fire. 'That's quite an accomplishment,' he murmured.

Tana nodded silently, so deep in thought that she didn't notice when he turned his head to look over his shoulder at her.

Her hair was loose and curly around her face, deeply black closest to her head, the top strands lightened by the fire and standing up and away from the rest like filaments of electricity in the dry heat. The flames she watched planted flickering, yellow sparks in the deep brown of her eyes, making her appear watchful, almost feral, when in fact she was completely relaxed.

'What are you thinking about?' Cody asked quietly.

Tana blinked, let her drifting mind catch up to the question, then focused on the man-shadow backlit by the fire. 'I was thinking about our first year here, before my mother died.'

His face was in shadow, but she didn't have to see his expression to feel his sympathy. 'Your mother died here?'

She nodded shortly, feeling a remnant of the old bitterness wash over her once again. 'She wouldn't have, if we'd been closer to a hospital.

His exhaled 'ah' was more a statement of understanding than any words of commiseration could have been, and she had the feeling he knew exactly why she had left this place, how earnestly and how long she had blamed the mountains and this ranch for her mother's death, and now, more recently, for her father's. And yet, somehow, this past week had diminished the bitterness a little. It surprised her to realise that she was no longer thinking of the ranch merely as the place that had killed her parents. She was beginning to think of it as home again.

She glanced around the large, dimly lit room with a faint smile, absorbing all the details that marked it as a ranch house—the wide planked floor, untroubled by the scuffing of boots, the huge, twisted-rag rugs almost impervious to wear and time, the massive pieces of leather furniture, as oblivious to fashion as they were to the dust on the seat of a visiting rancher's jeans. Everything as durable and timeless as man could make it. The room could have belonged in the nineteenth century or the twentieth—things had changed so little—but it definitely belonged here, in the shelter of the Montana mountains; the one place where time seemed to stand still and wait for man to catch up.

Her gaze shifted to Cody when he rose to his feet and moved to a big armchair to the left of the couch. Even he seemed part of this peculiar time-warp, dressed in clothes not unlike what cowboys had worn a hundred years before—faded jeans that had long since found the joints and musculature of his legs, scuffed boots with the telltale pristine heel of a rider, rather than a walker, and the standard denim shirt that paled beneath the intense blue of his eyes.

Now that she thought of it, she was the only thing in this room that seemed out of sync, wearing a full-length hostess dress that clearly belonged in the Chicago high-rise apartment where it had been worn most often. Although it was modest enough with its high mandarin collar and long, full sleeves, the soft fabric moulded provocatively to breast and hip, and dammit, she had known that very well. She'd also known that the deep rose colour picked up the natural blush in her cheeks, that the brushed velvet invited touch, that the tiny pearl buttons dancing from collar to hem accentuated the swell of breast and the dip of waist. So what had she been thinking of? That she would show him what he was missing? Advertise her femininity and play on the physical attraction he'd at least had the honesty to admit?

She glanced down at the dress self-consciously, mortified now by the apparent coldness of her sub-conscious calculation. Why hadn't Hazel said something when she'd come down for supper? Why hadn't she told her that the dress was totally unsuitable? That it made her motives painfully, shabbily obvious?

And the worst of it was that the last thing she really wanted was to succeed in a simple physical seduction. What she felt for Cody went much deeper than that. Somehow it was all tied up with this house, this ranch, this part of the country and the people who populated it; and her apparent intent to seduce him somehow cheapened the feeling.

She blushed as she came to that realisation, and was almost ready to make an excuse to go to her room and change when his words stopped her.

'You look lovely in that colour.'

She certainly hoped so, because now every exposed inch of skin was turning exactly the same shade.

'It was a silly thing to wear. I was just about to go change.'

'Why? Because it isn't denim or buckskin?' He'd leaned forward to rest his forearms on his knees and was smiling at her.

'Maybe,' she said, looking away, biting her lower lip because she could still feel his eyes on her. 'These are Chicago clothes.'

'Then let's hear it for Chicago,' he said quietly.

She turned her head towards him, suspicious of the compliment, only dimly aware of the clatter Hazel was making in the distant kitchen. It receded even further into the background when her eyes connected with his, and her lips parted involuntarily. There was something different in his expression—a clearness in the eyes, as if he'd just opened a door.

'I lost my folks to this land, too,' he said softly, and

she was so preoccupied with the clamour of her pulse that it took a moment for his revelation to sink in. All week she and Hazel had been probing for hints of his past, something that would flesh out the two-dimensional man living with them, and now, all of a sudden, he was volunteering information without any prompting at all.

She remained motionless, every sense alert.

'Of course, that was a long time ago. I was just a teenager, but I remember thinking that if we'd only lived somewhere else, somewhere flat, where the mountains don't twist the roads into corkscrews, where cars can't plummet a hundred feet or more before they hit the bottom, that my parents wouldn't have died. I blamed this country for years, just like you did.'

He reached over to smooth the line where Tana's brows had come together in sympathy, and also in the stunning realisation that he understood her completely. 'We need to blame *something* when we lose the things we love. But you and I blamed something that had always been part of us—the land—and so we hurt ourselves even more, by turning our backs on something we loved almost as much as the people we lost.'

'You did that, too?' she whispered.

Cody smiled sadly and nodded, and was about to say something else when Hazel entered the room, glasses rattling on a big aluminium tray. She stopped dead when she sensed the importance of the conversation taking place by the fire, and cursed herself silently for her poor sense of timing.

'What am I interrupting?'

Cody leaned back in his chair and smiled at her. 'A conversation that was getting much too serious,' he said.

'And brandy is just what we need to lighten the mood.'

Although initially Tana was reluctant to have that serious mood altered, the longer the three of them sat together by the fire, warmed by the brandy and relaxed by its effect, the more she began to wonder if life itself hadn't been just a bit too serious lately. Shattered by her father's sudden death, stunned by the prospect of losing the ranch, her emotions had been so tightly drawn for so long that it only occurred to her now that she'd almost forgotten how to laugh, and that laughter in itself was a great healer.

Hazel's first sip of brandy started her reminiscing about Brandy James, a ranch-hand so thin he'd been mistaken for a fence-post once when he was stretched out asleep, and only woke up just in time to save himself from being pounded into the ground; and from there her stories unwound from a spool of silliness, testing the limits of the wildest imagination, until even Cody laughed out loud.

'There,' Hazel grunted with satisfaction, apparently content with her achievement. 'High time we had some laugher in this house. Been nothin' but doom and gloom for too long now . . .'

Still flushed with brandy and laugher, eyes moist and lips frozen in the last smile, three heads turned abruptly at the sound of the heavy front door slamming shut.

'Tana!' A totally unexpected bass voice rumbled through the sudden silence of the house. In the fireplace, a hot ball of sap exploded in an exclamation point. 'Tana! I'm back!'

CHAPTER TEN

ZACHARY appeared as a dark, looming shadow in the broad archway that led to the front hall. He wore a black snowmobile suit that whistled when he took a step into the room, and a shiny black helmet that concealed all but the oval of his face. His heavy arctic boots were still crusted with white, as were his lower legs.

It was the way he was dressed, Tana decided instantly, that made his presence seem so forbidding, and surely it was only the lack of light in the room that made his eyes look so flat and empty. They had all turned in their seats at his entrance, but when he stopped just inside the archway he looked only at her.

'Zach,' she said, rising like a rose apparition from the couch, her dress rustling in the quiet as she turned to face him. Her voice sounded strangely hollow, as if she hadn't been sure what emotion to colour it with, and finally decided just to leave it blank.

'Tana.' That was all he said. She trembled a little at the way he was looking at her, as if nothing and no one else in the room existed for him. He didn't acknowledge Hazel, and he didn't seem to notice Cody.

'Well, if it isn't Zachary.' Hazel's voice was oddly subdued as she moved her bulk quickly to turn on a lamp. 'Why don't you get back into the hall and take off those wet things? You're making a lake where you stand.'

Without turning his head from Tana, his eyes shifted to where Hazel stood, the shadows from the lamp she'd just turned on streaking her face, making it look old.

'Of course, Hazel,' he said quietly, then he turned and left the room.

Tana took a deep breath once he was out of sight, and fought the extraordinary impulse to grab her glass and toss back the rest of her brandy, wondering what on earth would make her even consider such a thing. She felt Cody's eyes watching her, even when Zach came back into the room.

She relaxed a little to see the usual faded jeans and checquered flannel shirt that the snowmobile suit had hidden. Freed from the helmet, his hair angled over his brow in a black slash. Now he looked like the old Zach—devastatingly, darkly handsome, but no longer threatening. She walked over to greet him with a smile.

'You came back,' she said, and the words were barely out of her mouth when he grabbed her hands, a familiarity that was totally out of character for him, and totally unexpected.

'You knew I would.' He'd spoken softly, but his words, and the deeper meaning behind them, carried easily throughout the room.

'I knew no such thing,' she said uneasily, acutely conscious of Cody somewhere on the other side of the room, witnessing a scene Zachary was playing for much more than it was worth. Suddenly her brows lifted as she realised that he *had* noticed Cody, and was busily creating the illusion of a relationship between them that he only wished were real. 'As a matter of fact, when we heard on the radio that the road through the pass had been closed, we assumed you'd spend the winter at your brother's. How is he, by the way?'

'Bedridden, in a cast up to his hip.' His fingers tightened around hers when she started to pull away. 'But I found someone to manage his ranch until he's better.' Suddenly his angular features were split by a warm, white smile that looked like the sun breaking out from behind a cloud, and Tana returned the smile helplessly, wondering what foolishness could have made her uneasy in the first place.

'Tana,' he smiled tenderly, releasing her hands, touching her cheek gently, 'nothing would have kept me from coming back. I would never have left you alone here for the winter.'

'She's not alone,' Hazel broke in, 'as any fool can plainly see. Besides me, there's Cody. Douglas Cody, meet Zachary Chase, our foreman.'

There was no reason for the sudden electric tension that crackled between the two men when they looked at each other, but it was there nevertheless, like a jagged bolt of invisible lightning streaking across the room. At Hazel's introduction, Cody had risen to stand in the backlight of the fire, looking like some tall, blond god with an aura of flames around him.

Tana glanced at one man, then the other, thinking that the contrast between them would never be as evident as it was now, with Zachary standing darkly in the shadows, and Cody framed in light.

'A bed-and-board hand, I take it,' Zach said. Although his words were harmless, Tana was close

enough to Zach to see the convulsive tightening of jaw
and eyes that was the equivalent of an animal raising
its hackles. 'I didn't think there were any free hands
around this late in the season.'

Cody lifted one broad shoulder in an almost imperceptible shrug. 'Truth is,' he drawled, 'I hadn't
planned on any ranch work this winter. The storm
sort of talked me into it.'

Zach nodded, his eyes still fixed on Cody's, and
Tana had the oddest impression that everything about
him—his eyes, his hair, his complexion—seemed to
darken in that moment.

'Why don't we all sit down?' she asked lightly,
moving to turn away, stopping when she realised that
the men's concentration on each other was so intense
that neither had heard her. 'I said,' she repeated
succinctly, 'why don't we all sit down?'

Neither man moved.

Tana glanced across the room at Hazel, saw her lift
her brows and shoulders helplessly, but she too kept
silent.

'Well,' Zach broke the tension by rocking back on
his heels and jamming his thumbs into the front
pockets of his jeans, but he never took his eyes from
Cody, 'sorry you got stuck here when you weren't
planning on it, but it relieves me to know there was a
man here to fill in for me while I was gone.'

Tana bristled instantly at the clear implication that
she and Hazel were somehow under his care, but the
lingering undercurrent of hostility in the room kept
her from saying anything. Besides, the ranch, at least,
had been under Zach's care for almost a year, and he'd
worked hard and selflessly during that time with-

out expecting a thing in return. If he wanted to believe they couldn't function without him, what was the harm?

Cody's mouth twisted in a lazy smile, and to Tana's everlasting amazement he looked her thoroughly up and down before winking at Zach in lewd innuendo. 'Believe me, it was my pleasure.'

Zach was just sucking in a huge breath that was bound to explode when Hazel interrupted hurriedly. 'Come on, Zach. Pour yourself a measure of that brandy and bring it into the kitchen while I throw together something hot for you to eat.'

Zach continued to stare at Cody for a moment, then turned to Hazel, touching his forehead as if he were still wearing a hat. 'Appreciate it, Hazel. It's been a long trip.' He glanced briefly at the fireplace, then back at Cody. 'Could use some more logs on that,' he said pointedly, then he followed Hazel out to the kitchen.

Tana glared at Cody from across the room after they'd left, then stalked over to the fireplace, her skirt billowing behind her like an angry rose cloud. She pushed past Cody, knelt at the hearth, and started throwing logs on to the fire.

He leaned one elbow on the fieldstone above her and shifted his weight to his good leg. As he looked down at her kneeling at his feet, his face reflected satisfaction at the arrangement, and his eyes sparkled with mischief. Amusement exaggerated his drawl. 'Well, now, little lady. What're you so mad about?'

'Don't call me "little lady"!' she snapped, spinning her head to glare up at him, furious at the light of mockery she saw in his eyes. 'And you know perfectly well what I'm mad about! Heaven knows what he thinks has been going on here for the past week, and that's what you wanted. You're goading him!'

'Maybe.'

The admission surprised her, and her hand stopped half-way to another log as she looked up with a puzzled expression. 'Why?'

It bothered her that he just stared down at her without moving, without saying anything, and then it bothered so much that she felt a flush rising from beneath her dress to creep up her neck. Suddenly desperate to put an end to the silence and his stare, she repeated herself. 'Why?'

He smiled as if they'd been having a contest, and she lost because she spoke first. 'Let's just say the man rubs me the wrong way. Struck a spark the minute I got a look at him.'

'That's stupid.' She went back to piling logs on the fire. 'You sound like Hazel, hating the man without even knowing why.'

Out of the corner of her eye she saw the rise and fall of the toe of his boot as he flexed his healing ankle. 'Well, you can dress a rattlesnake up in top hat and tails, and you can give him a walking stick and teach him to sing the national anthem . . .' he looked down and smiled just as she looked up '. . . but people like Hazel and me are still going to know he's a rattlesnake.'

'Ah!' Tana shot to her feet, blew in exasperation at a black curl dangling over her forehead, then stalked over to the couch and sat down in an angry flounce. 'You're wrong about Zach. Both of you.'

'Hope so.' He was looking at her, but he wasn't

smiling any more. After a moment, he dropped to his heels and started to rearrange the mess she'd made of the fire. 'You didn't tell him about getting the cows down,' he said over his shoulder.

Tana folded her arms under her breasts. 'Hazel will tell him. Hazel will *love* telling him. Sometimes I think she lives just to make Zach mad.'

Cody half turned in his crouch to look at her. 'He thinks of this place as his,' he said quietly. 'Why would he be mad that you found a way to save it?'

'Number one,' Tana ticked off points impatiently on her fingers, 'he'll be furious that I went up into the mountains alone; number two, he'll be even more furious when he finds out you and I spent the night up there together; and number three, he'll feel cheated that he didn't save the place himself. Single-handedly. With one arm tied behind his back and his eyes taped shut.'

Cody chuckled and turned back to fire. 'And number four,' he added softly, 'you won't be trapped into marrying him any more.'

Tana sucked in a soft, startled breath. 'I was never trapped into marrying him.'

'You mean you wanted to?'

Tana opened her mouth, closed it, then opened it again, but before she had a chance to reply Hazel and Zach had come back into the room.

'Thought I'd eat in here by the fire,' Zach said as he folded himself into an armchair, a bowl of warmed stew in one hand, a plate of bread in the other. 'If I'm not interrupting, of course.'

'I've been telling Zach how crazy he was,' Hazel grumbled as she settled herself next to Tana on the couch. She carried a big tapestry bag and proceeded to dig into it while she talked. 'Travelling that many miles cross-country on one of those fickle machines . . .'

Zach smiled as he swallowed a mouthful of stew. 'Snowmobiles aren't nearly as fickle as horses, Hazel, and they're a hell of a lot faster.'

Hazel scowled into the tangle of yarn and needles she'd pulled from the bag. 'You know damn well we have avalanches in that pass every winter. You're just lucky the vibration didn't bring the whole mountain down on top of you.'

'As a matter of fact, there was a bit of a snowslide.' He smiled when he heard Tana's soft gasp. 'After I went through, the whole thing came tumbling down behind me.'

'You see? Plain crazy, just like I said!'

'Maybe.' He paused and glanced meaningfully at Tana. 'But I had to get back. Had to make sure things were all right here.'

It was almost more than Tana could take, this constant reminder that men out here still believed women were frail, helpless creatures in need of constant coddling. Frail? Helpless? She'd brought the cows down, hadn't she? And then she'd picked one man out of the dust while another gallivanted all over the country, and still they thought she was some silly, useless piece of ornamental fluff propped on the couch for their viewing pleasure. She scowled at Zach, and then Cody, who were facing one another in opposing armchairs like two stags in the spring rut.

'Things here are just fine,' she snapped at Zach, and felt the couch move with Hazel's silent chuckle. 'As a matter of fact, they're better than fine.'

Zach's spoon paused over his bowl. 'Is that right?'

'They saved the ranch,' Hazel said quietly, looking down at her knitting to hide her smile.

Zach hadn't moved—one booted ankle still rested comfortably on his other knee, his hands were still relaxed around his bowl—but the smile he'd been wearing seemed suddenly frozen on his face, and he had the air of a man who had just gone rigid after a heavy blow from an unexpected source. His eyes fixed on Hazel's for a moment, then darted to Cody, then Tana, then back to Hazel again. 'How's that?' he asked.

Hazel shrugged with feigned nonchalance as her eyes dropped back to her knitting. 'Tana went up into the mountains, then Cody here came along and went after her, and the next day they came down with Pillar and all those bred cows right behind them. They're in the loafing shed right now, and after the spring breeding-stock auction there'll be enough money to pay off D.C. and make a new start. Now, how's that for things being all right?'

For just an instant, Zach looked as if all the wind had been knocked out of him. 'I can't believe it,' he whispered, jerking his head to stare at Tana. 'You went up into those mountains?' She winced as his voice grew louder. She'd expected a scolding, not a firestorm. 'With a blizzard coming?' Now both his feet dropped to the floor with a thump and he leaned towards her and shouted, 'After what happened to your father, you went up there and brought those damn cows down . . .?'

'She was perfectly safe,' Cody interjected with a quiet voice, his own calmness emphasising Zach's loss of control, calling attention to it, humiliating him with it. 'I was with her.'

Tana, eyes still wide from Zach's unexpected outburst, felt Hazel nudge her with an elbow, and forced her head to turn and look at Cody. He was still slouched motionless in his chair, but his immobility had taken on the ominous characteristics of a tightly coiled spring, ready to explode.

'Not that she needed me, of course,' he went on, watching Zach carefully. 'As it turned out, I was the one thrown like a greenhorn, and she ended up taking care of me. Wouldn't doubt that these ladies are beginning to think men are more trouble than they're worth.'

Tana looked at Cody with something like amazement.

Zachary blinked, swallowed, then took a long time putting his used dish on the table next to his chair before he spoke again. 'So. The cows are down.'

'That's right.' Cody released a breath and his mouth curved in a lazy smile, but his eyes remained vigilant. 'Safe and healthy, every one, and wintering well, from what I can see.'

'Well.' Zach forced himself against the back of his chair and looked over at Tana. 'Well,' he repeated, 'that's certainly good news, isn't it, and as long as you're down safe . . .' He looked around idly, as if he couldn't quite remember what it was he was going to say, then slapped his knees with a suddenness that made Tana jump. 'Think I'll head on up to bed, if you don't mind. I'm just about done in.'

And suddenly he looked it. Tana's face softened as she saw the lines of strain pulling down his mouth, the dark stubble of beard shading his jaw. Foolish bravado or not, his long ride through the snowy night really had been an act of heroism, prompted by concern for the people who were important to him. She reached over and touched his knee in a gesture of gratitude, feeling guilty for ever being angry with him in the first place.

'I'm glad you're back, Zachary,' she said quietly.

He covered her hand with his and smiled wryly. 'Well, that's something, isn't it?' And then he left the room.

It was the first time she'd seen him, if not humble, at least subdued. That veneer of blustering masculinity had cracked, just a bit, and the glimpse of the vulnerable man beneath touched her. If only he could show a little more of that side . . .

'Tana.'

She turned her head slowly and blinked at Cody.

'I want to see the books.'

'The books?' she echoed stupidly.

'The ranch books.'

'Oh. They're in Dad's office, in the big desk.' She shrugged mindlessly. 'Help yourself. I think I'll . . .'

'Oh my, look at the time,' Hazel said suddenly, jumping to her feet so quickly that her yarn tumbled from her lap to the floor. 'Think I'll be getting up to bed, too. Night, Tana.' She kissed her noisily on the cheek. 'Night, Cody.'

'Goodnight, Hazel.' He glanced at her quickly, then back at Tana, almost as if he was afraid to take his eyes off her.

Tana rose wearily to follow Hazel up to bed, but before she'd taken a single step Cody was out of his chair, his hands spinning her around by the shoulders. Her eyes flew wide and she gaped up at him.

'You really *did* want to marry him, didn't you?' he demanded angrily, taking her completely by surprise.

'What? Wha . . .'

He shook her once, hard. 'And he really knows what buttons to push to get just what he wants . . .'

'Stop it!' She jerked free of his hands and took a couple of steps backward, and it was only then that she took a good look at his face, and had the sense to be alarmed by what she saw there. 'What are you talking about? What's the matter with you?'

'The way you looked at him,' he said menacingly, 'the way you *touched* him——'

She couldn't help it. One of her brows shot up speculatively before she could control it. 'Douglas Cody,' she murmured, lips curving into a mocking smile, 'I thought Zachary was the one who was supposed to get jealous . . .'

Before she could finish her sentence his arm snaked out in a blur of motion, snatching at the back of her neck, jerking her towards him, stopping her breath in her throat; then both hands were digging into the mass of her hair, holding her head immobile while his mouth crushed hers in a frantic, breathless kiss that left her knees weak and her whole body trembling.

'Cody . . .' she gasped when he finally released her, staring up into eyes that had almost disappeared between narrowed lids.

'You're playing a very dangerous game.' His voice rippled like the barely audible growl of an extremely large cat. She felt him circle her neck with one hand, and shivered when his thumb pressed lightly against the pulse in her throat. 'And-you're-going-to-get-hurt.'

'Who's going to hurt me?' she whispered thickly, raising her large eyes to gaze into his.

There was a sudden, spasmodic tightening between his blond brows. 'I am.'

'No.' She was almost giddy with a sudden sense of power, her eyes moist and glowing, her smile hypnotic in its certainty. 'No,' she repeated. 'You would never do that.'

This time his hands were gentle as they cradled her face, his lips tender, cherishing, as they nipped softly at hers. She would have collapsed against him if he hadn't shifted his hands to hold her by the shoulders. 'Tana, Tana,' he whispered brokenly. 'I won't be able to help it.' And then he turned and walked away, and left her staring after him in absolute astonishment.

CHAPTER ELEVEN

TANA lay on her back in the old four-poster that had been hers for as long as she could remember, and willed the dark rectangle of her bedroom window to lighten. Tension had followed her to bed each of the four nights since Zach's return, disturbing her sleep, waking her well before dawn.

'There's going to be trouble with those two living under the same roof,' Hazel had warned the morning after Zach's arrival. 'I can feel it.' And, although Tana had felt it too, she was more troubled by Cody's dark prophecy than Hazel's. He was going to hurt her, he'd said, and he wouldn't be able to help it. Now what on earth was that supposed to mean? She'd been walking an emotional tightrope ever since, waiting for the pro-verbial axe to fall, but the worst Cody had done in the past four days was to ignore her.

Maybe that was it, she thought, rolling on to her side, squeezing her eyes tightly shut, straining for a last few precious moments of sleep that refused to come. Maybe that was what he'd meant: that with Zachary back all interaction between them would stop.

But it hadn't. Not really. She smiled into the dark and pressed the button in her mind that called up a series of images from the past few days. Cody sprawled on a kitchen chair, chin on his chest, stunning her with the blue lash of his eyes when she happened to glance his way; Cody standing in the narrow doorway of the loafing shed, turning sideways to let her pass instead of moving out of her way, knowing that she would have to brush against him to get by; Cody watching with a fierce intensity whenever she and Zach exchanged words, as if his eyes could pierce her expression to see the thoughts behind it . . .

She flopped on to her back and took several deep breaths. There had been no moments alone, no physical contact, no thoughts verbalised and shared since Zachary had come back; but, if anything, the deprivation of those things seemed to intensify the attraction between them. Always, even when he was occupied with something else, she felt his awareness of her like a heavy, possessive hand on her heart.

In spite of Hazel's sense of foreboding, there had been no confrontations between the two men; at least, not openly. On the rare occasions when they spoke to each other, Tana had the strange sensation of something dark and powerful rumbling in the distance, warning of things yet to come; but so far they seemed to be operating under the terms of a reluctant, unspoken truce. Each morning and night they worked together in the loafing shed like two halves of a silent, efficient machine, with the exhausting pace of a contest that was never acknowledged, but existed none the less. After the first morning Tana resigned herself to the role of an idle supervisor, since there was no way she could match the quiet explosions of energy as the two men tossed the heavy bales of hay like feathers in the wind. She still accompanied them out to the shed, busying herself with chipping ice off the water tanks, checking individual cows for signs of disease or injury, but she had become little more than a figurehead, and she knew it. Cody and Zachary were testing each other, and she was the audience.

Last night had been the first indication that the testing period was over, that the tension of the past days was nearing the breaking point, threatening to explode.

She flung her arms out to the side and stared up into the blackness, remembering the way the two men had faced one another in front of the living-room fire while Hazel and Tana looked on warily.

'Just what are you trying to say?' Zach's eyes had been black sparks in the rigidly set framework of his face as the two men stood less than a foot apart, the fire snapping behind them.

'What I've said from the start,' Cody replied tightly, his eyes fixed on Zach's face. 'Everett Mitchell knew what he was doing. He was a good rancher. This place shouldn't have failed.'

The implication, of course, was that Zachary had somehow mismanaged the ranch, and Tana sat stiffly on the couch, holding her breath, waiting for Zach to defend his honour with his fists. Her own reaction to Cody's thinly veiled accusation was muddled. Part of her wanted to believe that her father *had* planned for any contingency; that, had he not been bedridden, Mitchell Ranch would still be solvent and productive—but, to believe that, she had to accept that Zachary Chase had been less than competent, and she simply didn't want that to be so. He'd tried so hard, given so much, cared so deeply—it just wouldn't be fair if that kind of effort had actually caused failure.

'It was a bad year for every ranch in this county,' she put in timidly, her eyes darting from one man's face to the other.

'Maybe,' Cody said flatly, still watching Zach. 'But this place has survived bad years before. Lots of them. Personally, I'm curious to learn why this year was so different. And I intend to do just that.'

Tana sat up in bed quickly, her stomach tightening in a replay of last night, still astonished that Zachary had somehow managed to control his volatile temper, and had simply replied, 'I hope you do. If there were mistakes made, maybe we can learn from them. Keep the same thing from happening again.' And then he had turned silently and gone up to bed. It was the reaction of a controlled, pacifist man, and because Zach had always been anything but that it seemed more ominous than a loss of control would have been. Even Hazel had been stunned into silence.

'You don't know him,' Tana had told Cody. 'He'll never forgive you for that.'

And then, if Zachary's behaviour hadn't been baffling enough, Cody's last words of the evening confused her more than ever. 'I know him better now,' he murmured to no one in particular, looking off across the room, 'and I almost made a mistake. He's smarter than I thought.'

The faint click of Hazel's door opening down the hall made Tana fling back the covers and slide from bed. She showered and dressed quickly, then gratefully left the solitary thoughts of her bedroom behind.

'They're going to kill each other.' Hazel was holding a huge pottery bowl against her side, beating furiously at the contents with a metal whisk. Neither man had come downstairs yet. 'Maybe not today, and maybe not tomorrow, but those two men are a fight waiting to happen. You mark my words.'

'If there was going to be a fight, it would have happened last night, Hazel, and it didn't.' Tana was leaning with her elbows braced against the kitchen counter, her legs crossed at the ankle. She eyed her stub-heeled cowboy boots reflectively, considering for a moment how androgynous the garb of the range was. Man or woman, daylight found them all dressed the same, in snug jeans and close-fitting shirts and boots that paid no mind to gender. No wonder the women out here jumped into dresses the moment night fell, as if they were panic-stricken that their femininity might be forgotten. She tugged absently at a coil of black hair curled over her shoulder.

'There *is* going to be trouble,' Hazel was insisting. 'At first I just thought it was two men fighting over the same woman . . .'

Tana made a face at her. 'Well, I'm glad you got past that idea, because if those two are fighting over a woman, it's got to be you. I've never felt more like an outsider in my life.'

'That's what I mean.' Hazel nodded thoughtfully. 'Those two are so wrapped up in whatever's festering between them, they hardly seemed to notice anything else. You been watching them when they're in the same room? Like a pair of mad bulls locked in the same paddock, each waiting for the other to make a move.'

Tana made a face at her. 'Cody accused Zach of running this place into the ground. It's no wonder Zach hates him.'

'He hated him a long time before that, Tana, and the feeling was mutual. Enemies on sight, that's what they were; as if they both recognised each other, or saw something in each other, and knew from the start that eventually they'd have to fight it out.'

Tana jumped when Zach appeared suddenly in the doorway. 'Morning, Hazel.'

He didn't greet Tana directly, but he didn't have to. She was the only thing he saw, and the message in his eyes was clear enough.

She'd been so caught up in the unspoken contest between the two men for the past few days that she'd almost forgotten how powerful Zach's attention could be when it was focused on her alone. The intensity of his black gaze was so hypnotic that she couldn't make herself look away from it.

'Morning, Zach,' she mumbled with uncharacteristic nervousness. 'Ready to go outside?'

He glanced around the room without moving his head. 'Cody isn't down yet?'

'Not yet.'

'Well,' Zach looked straight at her, 'I guess we can start without him.'

Tana faltered a little on her way to the back cloakroom, suddenly realising that she didn't want to go out to the shed alone with Zach, wondering what in the world would make her feel that way. She jumped when Zach closed the door behind him, effectively isolating them in the little room filled with coats and boots and scarves and the pungent aroma of barn. The kitchen noises receded into the background.

'What's wrong, Tana?' His hand rested on the hook that held his parka, and his brow puckered in a frown.

'Nothing,' she said with a quick smile, grabbing her coat and shrugging into it with a shiver. 'It's just cold out here.'

'No.' He reached out to touch her arm. She would have jumped back instinctively if his expression hadn't been so innocent, so puzzled. 'It's more than that,' he said quietly, searching her eyes. 'You're different this morning, almost as if . . . you were afraid of me.' His brows tipped in wounded disbelief, and suddenly the dark, rugged face transformed to that of an uncertain young boy. He pressed his lips together in a white line of frustration, and his voice was bitterly petulant. 'It's what Cody said last night, isn't it? He didn't say it right out, of course, he's too clever for that; but he planted the seed, and you believed him. You think I mismanaged the ranch . . .'

Tana's mouth dropped in a surprised circle, because in truth what had been said last night had nothing to do with the way she was feeling now. 'Zach, I wasn't thinking any such thing. I . . .' She looked down at her boots as if they could give a satisfactory answer for why she was so suddenly uncomfortable with a man she'd known for years. 'I don't know what's the matter with me this morning, Zach,' she sighed finally. 'I'm just on edge, I guess. You and Cody . . .'

'Me and Cody what?' His eyes narrowed suspiciously.

Tana looked up at him, suddenly irritated that she was allowing her uncertainties to show; angry with Zach, and with Cody too, for putting her so off balance. 'You hate each other, that's what,' she said sharply, 'for no good reason that I can see, and it's making us all tense. It's like living with an unexploded bomb.'

His face cleared like a sunrise pushing back the dark, and his strong, chiselled features were tempered with a charming vulnerability. 'Oh', he said sheepishly, and the beauty of his smile dazzled her, almost made her forget what they'd been talking about, 'so that's it.' He dropped his head and chuckled, then pulled his coat from the hook and slipped it on. 'Of course we hate each other. What did you expect? We're in competition for the same woman.'

Tana's lips parted on a word that was immediately lost to her, and all she could do was blink. She hadn't expected to hear Hazel's first assessment of the situation confirmed so readily. It just wasn't like Zach to be so open about his feelings. There was too much risk in that for a proud man. True, he'd 'offered' to marry her, to give her a home when it was obvious the Mitchell Ranch was going to be lost; but the offer had sounded more like charity than a proposal, and that was the way he'd wanted it. Then if she turned him down it wouldn't really be a rejection of him personally—just a rejection of his charity. But this—this startling admission that he was actually competing for her—he was leaving himself wide open, and that wasn't like him.

He pretended to be preoccupied with zipping up his coat, but then he raised his head slowly until his eyes met hers. They were black and bottomless and, incredibly, they looked hot. 'Why do you look so surprised, Tana? You've always known how I felt about you.'

She heard the sound of her fingernail plucking nervously at the zipper of her coat, but she couldn't take her eyes from his. There was something wrong here; something slightly off-kilter.

He started to pull on one mitten, then changed his mind and stuffed it into his jacket pocket instead. 'I've never been very good at putting things into words, I guess,' he said slowly, staring at her. 'I always thought that when things were right between a man and a woman, they both just . . . knew. But maybe I was wrong . . .'

She was almost unaware of him moving closer, cupping her chin in one rough hand, tipping her face upwards. She felt his breath stir her eyelashes. It was such a gentle, harmless kiss; certainly not the kind of gesture one would insult with rejection. By then, before she knew it, the pressure of his mouth became fiercely demanding, his breath frantic, and he was pushing her bodily against the wall, pinning her there. She was so flabbergasted by the unexpected aggression that all she could do was laugh weakly when she finally managed to twist her head to one side. 'Zach, what are you doing?' she gasped, irritated that her voice had sounded more coy than indignant.

'Good question.'

The door banged against the outside wall when Cody entered, the furred edge of his parka rimmed with frost, his eyes cold flashes of blue in a reddened face.

'Cody!' Tana whispered, backing away from Zach like an embarrassed schoolgirl, tugging her parka back into place. She searched Cody's face for an indication of how he was interpreting the scene he had walked in on, but his expression was unreadable. 'We thought you were still upstairs,' she said, and then wished immediately that she could call back the words that had sounded so lame.

His eyes darted in silence from her face to Zach's, then back again. 'I see,' he said drily. 'Then I take it I'm interrupting.'

'Damn right you are.' Zach's eyes glittered darkly in a face as rigid as stone.

Without understanding what prompted her, Tana stepped quickly between the two men, facing Cody. To

her frustration, he continued to look over her shoulder at
Zach. 'You did morning chores already?' she asked
weakly.

He nodded once, still staring past her at Zach. 'I
couldn't sleep. I went out early.'

'Well, then,' she said brightly, making a production of
removing her coat, 'that's terrific. We can eat breakfast
right away, then. Come on, Zach.' She tugged at his arm
once, and he ignored her completely; twice, and he
shook off her hand with the vicious thoughtlessness of a
horse flicking away a troublesome fly.

Tana stared at him while her hand dropped mindlessly to her side. He didn't even know she was there.
She jerked her head to look at Cody, but he didn't seem
to notice her either. In that moment she realised that
Zach had been lying. Whatever darkness existed
between these two men was rooted in something much
deeper than jealousy—something that had nothing to do
with her.

'Zach,' she insisted, and his eyes jerked to hers
abruptly, as if he'd suddenly remembered her presence.

'Right,' he mumbled sullenly, turning to take off his
coat and jam it so forcefully against the hook that Tana
wondered that it didn't jerk the screws right out of the
wall. Frowning in puzzlement, she watched him stomp
from the room and go back into the kitchen, slamming
the door behind him.

'What is it with you two?' she demanded of Cody,
attracting his attention at last. She couldn't be sure, but
she thought his face softened a little when he looked at
her.

'What do you think?' he asked cryptically, easing
down to the bench that lined one wall.

'I think you're both crazy, that's what I think,' she snapped, kicking at a stray boot that had somehow found its way to the middle of the floor. 'I think we should give you both loaded guns and lock you in a closet and let you get this over with. I think . . .'

'Tana.'

Something in his voice stopped what promised to be a full-fledged tirade, and made her turn to look at him. He was sitting on the bench with his knees spread, arms draped over his thighs, his head lifted to look at her. He'd pushed back the hood of his parka, and strands of wet-darkened blond cut across his forehead like fresh wounds. He looked tired.

'There's something very wrong here,' he said quietly.

She rolled her eyes and emitted a short, breathy laugh. 'No kidding.'

'I don't think you understand it yet.'

'Understand it?' she almost shouted. 'Of course I don't understand it! No one understands it! Hazel thinks you're a couple of mad bulls, Zach thinks he's got competition from a man who avoids me like the plague, you think you're on the trail of the mystery of the decade, and I . . .' Her shoulders slumped in frustration.

'Mad bulls?'

She shook her head and moved towards the door to the kitchen. 'Never mind.'

In the space of a heartbeat he had leaped from the bench and planted himself between her and the door. The move had been accomplished with such sudden violence that she took a quick step backwards, not knowing what to expect, but all he did was stand there, looking down at her. His arms were pressed stiffly against his sides, his face was expressionless, as if he couldn't trust himself to allow a single muscle in his body freedom to act. 'I want you to know,' he said woodenly, barely moving his lips, 'that I've done a lot of hard things in my life.' His nostrils flared slightly with an intake of breath that lifted his chest. 'But none as hard as being here for this past week, wanting . . . things . . . I had no right to.'

Tana felt the dryness of eyes opened too wide for too long, and blinked. The crisp smell of snow and cold emanated from his coat, surrounding her, drawing her into a small circle of reality that held them both, shutting out the rest of the world. His eyes were as eloquent as his expression was blank. They burned with the intensity of desperate longing; the pain of self-denial.

She watched her own hand move towards his face, wondering absently if she had engineered the movement, or if her body had finally shed the constraints of her mind in disgust. And, if that were the case, what was so bad about that? Weren't humans always messing up their lives by denying their instincts? Wasn't that what her father had always said? 'Don't think so hard about how to ride a bucking horse, Tana, or he'll throw you every time! Your body knows what's right. Listen to it!'

Yes, she thought silently, her eyes fixed on Cody's. Yes. Forget all the logic that tells you this man is a stranger, that there's no rational reason for that silent, vital bonding that's drawn you from the beginning; forget everything he's ever said and done that made you think he didn't want you, because none of that is real. Your body knows that, even if your mind hasn't figured it out yet. Listen to it!

And so she watched her hand tremble within an inch of the dark stubble on the line of his jaw, saw the quick intake of his breath that flared his nostrils, and knew that she was right. Her fingers trembled slightly when they finally made contact with his skin, then froze when he jerked his head back and slammed his eyes shut.

'Ta—na . . .' Her name escaped through his clenched teeth as he grabbed her hand and jerked it down, away from his face, unwittingly pulling her against him with the force of the motion. Her eyes flew wide at the impact of her body against his, and her head dropped back on her shoulders as she looked up at his face, her lips parted expectantly. His scowl was a fierce, furious effort to control that which was ultimately uncontrollable, and for a moment he was still master of the body that was betraying him. Even as his heart pounded so strongly that Tana could feel it through his jacket, he remained motionless, his hand imprisoning hers behind her back, his eyes drilling into hers. But, impressive as his outward control was, the force of his ragged breath betrayed him, and Tana shuddered at the swelling pressure of his chest rising against her breasts. Her eyes fluttered closed for just an instant, and it was then that he grabbed the back of her neck and with a low moan let the full force of passion too long restrained explode from his mouth to hers.

They came together with the bruising violence of cymbals, destined from the first white heat of forging to collide and meld in a noisy, magnificent union.

'Cody,' Tana gasped his name into his mouth, thinking she would never be able to breathe normally again, that whatever this raging, rising heat within her was, it must find release soon, or her body would explode.

'Tana,' he moaned helplessly, his hands on her face now, fingers threading into her hair, his lips moving

frantically over her mouth, freezing suddenly on her
cheek when a sharp sound penetrated the door to the
kitchen and reminded them both of where they were.

She felt the force of his held breath expend itself
against her cheek, and then his hands pushed her gently
away by the shoulders.

'Damn,' he breathed, his eyes dark between narrowed
lids, fixed on hers with an animal-like intensity. Her
mind couldn't read his eyes, couldn't put a name to what
she saw there, but she knew instinctively that her own
looked exactly the same.

For a moment they just stood there, making furious,
passionate love with their eyes while the room was filled
with the ragged sounds of their breathing, then suddenly
Cody squeezed his eyes shut and shook his head.

'For heaven's sake, Tana,' he gasped, taking a step
backward until he collided with the door. 'Get out.
Right now. Or I won't care who the hell walks in, or
what they see.'

She nodded mutely, watched every move as he walked
back over to the bench and sat down, then slipped
quickly through the door to the kitchen. Hazel was
leaning back against the sink, her arms crossed under
her breasts, her lips curved in a knowing smile. Tana's
eyes fell closed in relief when she saw that Zach was
nowhere in sight.

'He went straight upstairs after he slammed out of
there,' Hazel answered her silent question. 'Left you two
alone, fool that he is.' Her smile broadened slightly and
her brows arched. 'Child, you better splash some cold
water on that red face of yours and put the fire out.'

With the exception of an awkward, silent breakfast,

neither Hazel nor Tana saw either man for the rest of the day. Zach had been out on the tractor, clearing the huge paddocks with the snowblower attachment, and Cody had locked himself in her father's office with the books.

That was just as well, as far as Tana was concerned. She couldn't think when Cody was around—every time she looked at him her mind simply shut off while her body went into overdrive—and she needed to think about that most of all.

In spite of what her father had said, she still believed that instinct was something you obeyed only selectively —that was what separated man from the beasts, right? Yes, you should listen to your instincts when you were riding a bucking horse, or roping a wayward calf; even when you were trying to guess tomorrow's weather—but anyone who would trust their heart to another on the basis of instinct alone was just asking for trouble. That was when the process of logical thought counted most, when you could use it to assess a person, evaluate their worth and their motives, and respond accordingly.

But instinct was all she had to go on with Cody, because she really didn't know a thing about him. For all the time they'd spent together over the last two weeks, he was as much of a mystery man as he'd been the first moment she saw him.

Although it had never seemed that he was intentionally avoiding questions about his past or present life, he had somehow managed to reveal nothing of those mundane but telling details that made up the bulk of a man's life. It was almost as if he hadn't existed before he rode on to Mitchell property, and would cease to exist once he left it.

And yet, while her mind told her the man was a virtual stranger, and therefore not to be trusted, her mind didn't seem to be controlling the rest of her body very well. Where had her mind been in the cloakroom this morning? On vacation?

'Tana, you're going to pace the tiles right off the floor. Now get over here and sit down.'

Tana stopped in front of the sink and glanced over at Hazel sitting at the table. 'I think better when I pace.'

'Well, then, stop it. You always did think too much for your own good.'

'You sound just like Dad,' Tana smiled faintly, jamming her fingers into the front pockets of her jeans. She turned and peered out of the kitchen window into the cold night, and shivered in spite of the kitchen's warmth.

Even though it had been full dark for nearly an hour, a generous moon washed the snow with reflected light. A hundred yards distant, shadows of the paddock fence-posts lay in grey, jagged lines over the white drifts, as if a child had drawn them there. Beyond the paddocks the loafing shed loomed like a man-made mountain, darker than the night, cold and forbidding.

Tana stared at it, rubbing her arms under the heavy wool of her sweater, a line of worry marring her brow. 'We shouldn't have let them go out there alone, Hazel. There's going to be trouble.'

The older woman clucked her tongue and sighed. 'You've been babysitting those men for days now. Time they worked things out on their own. Besides, you're the rancher, remember? And they're the hands. You shouldn't have to be doing chores yourself anyway, as long as you got enough help. First sensible thing Zach's said since he came back, if you ask me.'

Tana stomped over to the table and plopped down hard in the chair next to Hazel. She pushed the heavy mass of her hair away from her face, then dropped her chin in her hands. The deep brown eyes were unnaturally bright with worry. 'That's what bothers me most, that it was Zach's idea. Now, why would he want to be alone out there with Cody?'

'To talk plain, I suppose,' Hazel shrugged. 'As I said, it's time those two worked out their differences.'

Tana made a face at her. 'This morning you said they were going to kill each other; now all of a sudden you think they're diplomats.'

Hazel chuckled and straightened the straps of her apron on her broad shoulders. 'I didn't say *how* they were going to work things out. As a matter of fact, my best guess is that one or both of them is going to come in a little more battered than when he went out . . .'

'What?' Tana's mouth dropped open and she went rigid. 'You think they're going to fight?'

Hazel blinked at her with a puzzled smile. 'Well, of course they're going to fight. They're cowboys, aren't they? And they hate each other, and what they both need is to get that venom out of their systems . . . hey! Where do you think you're going?'

Tana had jumped from her chair and was sprinting towards the cloakroom. Hazel blew out a sigh of exasperation, then rose wearily from her chair and followed.

'Tana,' she scolded gently from the doorway, 'leave them be. Sometimes it's the only way for two men to work out their differences. It's when they don't get a chance to work them out that there's real trouble.'

'Oh, Hazel!' Tana snapped, jamming her feet into snow boots, jerking on a bulky parka. 'Just because we live in the wilderness, it doesn't mean we have to act like animals!'

Hazel's eyes hardened slightly as she watched Tana struggle with the zipper on her coat. 'We're all animals,' she said quietly. 'Some of us just pretend better than others.'

Tana shot her an exasperated glare, then rushed out into the night.

The snow squeaked under her boots as she crossed the moonlit yard towards the huge shed, but that was the only sound she heard. No bloodcurdling screams splitting the night air; no frantic lowing of cows trying to dodge bodies falling from the loft. 'That's good, that's good,' she panted as she walked faster and faster, little clouds of condensed breath popping like frosty balloons from her mouth. 'Silence is good. That's a good sign.' She slammed her mouth closed when she realised she was talking to herself.

She was half-way to the shed, her nose already prickling with the cold, when she got angry all over again because she was back in that part of the country where men still argue with their fists. It was one of the few things she'd been completely content to leave behind when she'd moved to the city.

The heels of her boots jammed sharply into the snow as she recalled all the fights she'd seen growing up here; all the hot-headed, range-weary cowhands expending pent-up energy in an explosion of fists; fighting over the silliest things, looking for the slightest reason to strike out at one another, and then damn near revelling in the violence, like schoolboys in a sporting competition.

Although she'd never seen anyone seriously hurt, and though the fights had always had an almost circus-like air about them, she'd still found them senseless and frightening. Even worse than the fighters themselves were the people who often looked on, smiling complacently, nodding as if two men taking pokes at each other was part of the natural order of things. And what was even more frustrating was that you were apt as not to see two fierce combatants sharing a drink and a laugh afterwards, as if there had never been trouble between them at all.

'We depend on each other too much to let anger fester,' her father had told her once, trying to temper her fury when he'd let two of his hands battle it out in the yard. 'Now, those two boys had a serious bone to pick with each other, and so they did, and now it's done, and they can trust each other again. As you say, Tana, it may not be civilised, but sometimes I wonder if civilised behaviour isn't just a Band-aid on a festering wound. Can't heal every wound that way. Some of 'em just have to be opened up to the air.'

She stopped at the door to the shed and sighed, saddened to remember one of the differences that had pulled her and her father apart. She'd left the ranch shortly after that incident, determined to find a place in the world where the philosophy of the fist didn't prevail; and she'd found it, hadn't she? Never once in Chicago had she seen one man strike another, blacken an eye or bruise a jaw. They didn't do things that way in the city. Enmities were much more subtle. More civilised.

For some reason what Hazel had said popped into her mind without warning. 'We're all animals. Some of us just pretend better than others.'

Tana wiped her mitten across her face, as if she could erase the troubled thoughts that formed her expression, and stepped through the small doorway into the tractor drive-through. The only illumination came from a single bulb dangling far above her, and outside the beam of that light the alleyway was dark.

She smiled a little when she heard the comforting sound of a bale of hay hitting the loft floor above her, and then felt a little guilty for ever suspecting these two men would come to blows. She'd never seen Zach strike a man, even in the worst fit of temper; and Cody . . . somehow Cody seemed above such things. There were still civilised men, she comforted herself with a nod; even out here.

'All right, Cody.'

The sound of Zach's voice was muffled, but something in the tone made her catch her breath and hold it while her eyes rolled upwards, as if she could see through the loft floor. She eased the door quietly closed behind her and stood motionless beyond the glare of the single light, waiting.

'Let's get it settled.'

She heard the soft thud of something hitting the floor; heavy leather mittens, perhaps. She closed her eyes and strained to make out Cody's reply.

'It's not that simple, Zach. It's going to take more than a scuffle to settle what's between us.'

Tana allowed herself a brief sigh of relief.

'I don't think so.'

Her throat tightened again and she jumped as something else hit the floor above. Something larger than the last time. A coat?

Part of her wanted desperately to call up to the two

men, to defuse the argument before it turned into a fight; but another part reminded her that, in reality, this was none of her business. Zach and Cody were grown men, not children, and if there was bad blood between them they had every right to find their own solution without interference from her. And there was something else, too—some sixth sense that told her she could never be in the middle of what was happening between these two men. Before it was over, she would have to take sides, and she wasn't prepared to do that.'

'You're an outsider, Cody.' Zach's growl seemed to creep down the ladder towards her. 'You don't belong here. And I'm going to send you on your way, with something to remember me by.'

Tana's foot was on the bottom rung before she knew she intended to climb.

'And why should an outsider bother you, Zach?' Cody's voice covered the soft thumps of her boots ascending the rungs. 'Unless you're afraid an outsider can see the truth of what's been going on here . . .'

'I don't know what the hell you're talking about! The only thing going on here is that you want to move on Tana, and I'm not about to let you do it!'

There was a sudden silence, and Tana froze half-way up the ladder. She could hear the warning quiver in Cody's voice.

'This isn't just about Tana, Zach, and you know it. You damn near ran this place into the ground, and I'm going to prove it. *That's* what you're afraid of.'

'You son of a bitch!' Zach bellowed, and Tana scurried up the rest of the ladder until her head poked through the loft floor. Her mouth was open to shout at them to stop it, but the words froze in her throat when she saw that there was nothing to stop, at least not yet.

The two men were facing each other in the centre of the loft floor, each so intent on the other that they never noticed her in the shadows. Zach had shed his outer clothes and stood with his shoulders hunched inside a sweater as black as his tousled hair, his head belligerently forward on his neck, his fists clenched at his sides.

Cody still wore his mittens and parka, but he'd thrown the hood back. The feeble light from the loft ceiling danced on the crown of his head, making his golden hair seem more like a source of light than a recipient. 'I don't want to fight you, Zach,' he said steadily, but his posture was defensive, expectant. His legs were slightly spread, jeans tightly stretched over the tense muscles of his thighs, weight on the balls of his feet. Although his arms seemed relaxed at his sides, his elbows were bent slightly beneath the bulk of his coat. More than anything else, he looked like a tennis player about to receive a serve.

'Damn right you don't, you yellow bastard,' Zach sneered, 'but you're going to all the same.'

This time Tana didn't care whether it was her business or not. She wasn't about to hang on this ladder like some stupid, gape-mouthed spectator while these two men . . .

Zach moved before the shout reached her mouth, head down, charging like a bull, intent on driving Cody into the stack of hay bales behind him, and then suddenly it was over.

Tana stared in disbelief at the man who had been upright just seconds before, lying flat on his back on the dusty floor, knees raised, spine rolled forward, arms clutching his stomach while he gasped for breath. His face reflected absolute astonishment, and in that moment Tana realised that probably never in his life had Zach found himself lying helpless before another man.

It had all happened so fast that she felt as if she'd fallen asleep for a time, or missed an entire series of moves and counter-moves by fighters who battled too swiftly for the human eye to absorb.

Cody stood precisely where he had before, and except for the slight bend in his left knee and the upright position of his left arm, it would have been impossible to imagine that he had in any way been responsible for Zachary's current predicament. 'I'm not going to fight you, Zach,' he said with total composure. He looked down at the fallen man with the flat, empty gaze of a doll. 'I'm not going to prove you're a liar and a thief with my fists, and you're not going to stop me from finding the proof with yours. So let's end this now.'

Something made Tana duck down until only her eyes were visible through the opening in the loft floor. Her breathing was shallow and silent, and within her mittens the tips of her fingers grew white with the pressure of her hands on the ladder rungs. Zach? A liar and a thief? What was he talking about?

'Some day you'll pay for this,' Zach hissed through clenched teeth, stumbling to his knees, then rising slowly to his feet. He stood with a slight forward bend to his waist, his fists white and quivering at his sides. 'Some day soon, so help me, you'll pay.'

Tana felt a shiver crawl up her spine.

While Zach bent stiffly to gather his coat and mittens, she moved swiftly, silently, down the ladder, out of the door into the bitterly cold night, and across the yard towards the house.

CHAPTER TWELVE

TANA crept down the broad, dark staircase of the old house, the heels of her boots lifted to avoid waking anyone lucky enough to be asleep. She might be the only one prowling around well after midnight, but she suspected that she probably wasn't the only one awake. The last twenty-four hours had been fraught with tension, and sleep wasn't coming easily to anyone.

After yesterday's incident in the loafing shed, Zach's black mood had become almost palpable; so pervasive that it seemed diffused, directed at all of them, instead of just Cody. Seething, barely contained rage coloured his every glance and word, until now it seemed more a state of being than a single emotion. Zachary was not simply furious; Zachary was fury itself. Tana could only guess how much worse it might have been had he known she had witnessed his humiliation, let alone passed it on to Hazel.

The meals since had been a nightmare of awkward, crackling silence that Tana could only compare to those dead, ominous moments of stillness before a violent summer storm. Fortunately, those were the only times the four of them gathered together; otherwise Zachary kept very much to himself. Still, Tana was almost sick with fearful anticipation of catastrophe, pathetically grateful for each hour of this day that had passed without incident.

144

Of the four of them living in the winter-shrouded ranch-house, Cody was the only one seemingly untouched by the pall of Zach's seething hatred, even though he was its primary target. He watched the man who was his enemy with the bright, alert eyes of curious assessment, but neither fear nor trepidation clouded the blue gaze. If anything, his expression reflected a quiet contentment Tana had not seen before, as if he had identified a threat and, in so doing, disarmed it. He had been totally, incongruously relaxed on this day when everyone else had been rigid with tension, seemingly oblivious to Zachary's dark glances and Tana's and Hazel's skittering nervousness. The steady, forceful thump of his boots crossing a room had been oddly comforting on a day when everyone else strained to move from place to place in quiet oblivion, as if the sound of their passing would ignite an omnipresent fuse.

The only bright spot in an otherwise ominous day had been the restoral of phone service. They had all jumped at the almost forgotten jangle when the telephone rang during the early afternoon.

A short time after Zach had answered the kitchen extension, he walked into the living-room with a small smile that only served to accentuate the black, constant rage in his eyes.

'Just the phone company, checking the service,' he'd said, glancing at Cody, smiling strangely, then looking at Tana for an instant before he turned and left the room.

She shivered now, remembering the lash of malice in his dark eyes, the smug turn of his mouth. She'd spent the rest of the day trying to convince herself that Zachary had looked perfectly normal, that the strain of the day had made her read things into his expression that simply weren't there. And yet, try as she might to dispel the feeling, Zachary had frightened her in that moment, as if she'd caught a glimpse of something dark and unpleasant that she'd never been meant to see. Such a notion was ridiculous, of course; insupportable by logic, prompted only by pure, mindless instinct . . .

The thought gave her pause, and she stopped on the stairs, her expression troubled, her hand clutching the banister. There it was again. The old conflict between instinct and rational thought. Which one did you believe? If she justified her instinctive responses to Cody, could she really ignore her instinctive responses to Zach?

'Oh, to hell with it,' she muttered under her breath, stomping down the rest of the stairs. It was all too complicated to figure out at this hour, and this creeping around her own house, jumping at shadows, was just patiently ridiculous.

But the house itself felt strange to her—almost malevolent—and when she caught sight of a band of light under the door to her father's office she caught her breath and held it, her eyes widening when the door eased open silently, spilling a broad shaft of light on to the hall floor. Then Cody's blond head poked out and he squinted towards the stairs. He smiled when he saw her in the shadows.

'I thought I heard someone. Come on in.'

The doorway to her father's office had never seemed narrow, until Tana walked past Cody on her way in. In a strange way, she felt as if she were parading by some sort of a judge, and found herself wondering what she looked like in profile, how disordered the black tumble of her hair was, and if the lack of sleep showed on her face.

She stopped and turned as he closed the door quietly behind them. 'I couldn't sleep,' she explained, looking up at the faint lines of strain pulling at his fine, strong mouth, the pockets of shadow in the hollows just beneath his cheekbones.

The only light came from the green-shaded desk lamp across the room, and here, in the shadows, he looked more like a painting of a man than the real thing.

Looking down at her, he smiled suddenly, and his face came alive. Tana felt her heart turn over in her chest, setting off a chain reaction of physical responses she was absolutely powerless to control. Her lips parted and trembled slightly as she gazed up at him, and her eyes darkened and softened until they looked like warm, welcoming entryways lined with rich brown velvet. Looking into them, Cody's mouth tightened so strongly over a caught breath that his lips whitened, and he had to turn away.

'There's coffee over here on the desk,' he said, striding towards it in a sudden rush. 'Use my mug. I've had enough.'

Tana stayed motionless for a moment while her eyes followed him across the room. At the desk he stopped, half turned, and looked at her from a safer distance. She hesitated only an instant before moving towards him, but in her mind time stopped in that instant, and gave her the visual details of a picture that would live in her memory forever—the penetrating reach of his eyes, bluer than any eyes had a right to be; the way the fabric of his shirt strained across his shoulders; the slight spread of his legs; the musculature of forearms exposed by his rolled-up sleeves.

She blinked once, marvelling that she could even operate her eyelids, the lashes seemed so suddenly heavy, and then walked over to the desk. He watched her come towards him with an intensity that made her acutely aware of her own body, the mechanical motion of her legs inside her jeans, the steady rise of her breast beneath the thin blue cloth of a shirt that suddenly seemed too tight.

'Here.' He filled the mug he had used, and Tana took it wordlessly, looking down at where her finger touched tentatively at the rim, thinking that his mouth had been there. The thought made her flush, and she unconsciously reached up to cover the hot pulse at her throat.

'Sit down,' he told her, and she didn't even look up at him. She didn't dare do anything but reach blindly for the back of the chair that faced the desk, and ease herself slowly into it. Her jeans seemed to cut into her thighs and the backs of her knees as she sat, and it felt as if the snaps on her shirt were straining the cloth that connected them.

She gulped at the coffee like a woman dying of thirst, lifting her eyes warily only when she heard him move away from her, careful to look at anything but him. Her eyes settled on the stack of open ledgers spread across the desk. She tried to ignore the fact that he had sunk into her father's chair behind the desk, entering her line of vision. 'I see you're still fascinated with the ranch books,' she said quietly.

She couldn't help it. When he spoke, she had to look at him. 'They make fascinating reading,' he said, and she had to frown to remember what he was talking about. 'As a matter of fact, you're the one who should be studying them, not me.'

It was just a game. A game of words. They were just taking turns talking, pretending that only what they said had meaning, not what was passing between their eyes.

'I've never been one for book-keeping,' she said. 'Neither was Dad. Zach takes care of the books. He always has.'

She watched his eyes as they travelled over her face, touching her brows, her cheeks, her lips, then shifting to take in the dark halo of her hair. She saw the lift of his chest swelling with a great breath, then he looked down at the desk, picked up a pencil and began rolling it between his palms.

'You looked at the books when you found out you were about to lose the ranch,' he began hoarsely, stopping to clear his throat. 'What did they tell you?'

Don't look at him, she told herself. It took a monumental effort of will to drop her head and gaze into the mug of forgotten coffee. 'Only that we've had enormous expenses, and not a whole lot of income this past year.' She brought the mug to her lips and took a small swallow, then found herself looking directly across the desk to meet his eyes. Unwittingly, she smiled at him, watched with something like amazement as he smiled back, realising suddenly that he was responding to her as helplessly as she responded to him. The knowledge sent an unexpected wave of joy surging through her, leaving a reckless confidence in its wake.

'Why are you spending so much time on the books, Cody? It isn't important.' And indeed, it wasn't. It couldn't be. Nothing was important any more, except the way he looked at her, the certainty that he had finally torn down whatever barriers had stood between them.

'I told you,' he said thickly, staring at her, and more

than ever she felt that two conversations were taking place here, one in words, and one on a subterranean level of raw emotion that could never find expression in words alone, 'now that you've got a new start, you should find out where things went wrong, so you don't get in trouble again.'

'And that's why *I* should be studying the books. It doesn't explain why you're doing it.'

He closed his eyes and rubbed his hand across his mouth. She could hear the scrape of his palm on the stubble of his beard, and the sound rippled up her spine and down again.

Boldly, heedlessly, she closed the distance between them by leaning towards the desk, bracing her elbows on it, propping her chin in her hands. 'You care,' she murmured, entranced by the freedom of finally being able to give voice to her thoughts. 'You care about me, and Hazel, and the ranch, and our future, and for some reason you've been trying to hide that. Why?' She smiled and shook her head slightly, mystified. 'Is caring about others such a terrible thing? Is that the secret you've been guarding so carefully ever since you came here?'

She frowned when the strong face tightened, then crumpled as he dropped his chin to his chest. Something was wrong. Something she'd said was terribly wrong. 'Cody?' she whispered, leaning forward, dropping her hands to the desk, cursing herself for the unknown mistake that had shattered the mood, destroyed him so visibly, ruining everything.

He sagged a little as if her words had taken all the air out of him, then leaned across the desk and grabbed both of her hands in his. He looked down at the slender, graceful fingers cradled in his palms and sighed. 'I wonder why people always find irony so amusing,' he said bitterly, stroking his thumbs across her fingers, then raising his eyes to meet hers. 'I love this place, Tana. I belong here. That's my secret.'

Her brow cleared and her lips parted slightly in a radiant smile that began in her mind, and hadn't quite found its way to her mouth yet. Of course he belonged here. With her. 'I know that,' she whispered, the words tumbling over one another in her relief. 'I knew that the day we met. What I didn't know then is that I belong here, too. I think I always have, but you're the one who made me realise it.'

She didn't understand why his smile was so pained, why he wouldn't meet her eyes any more. 'And that's the irony,' he said with even more bitterness, then he spun violently in the chair and banged one fist on the desk. 'Dammit! I should have told you this long before now!'

Tana was frantic with confusion, her hands clenched into fists on the desk where he had dropped them, her frown desperate. Everything he said should have made things perfect between them, but instead he was reacting as if they would tear them apart, and she didn't know what to say.

'Cody?' she questioned him fearfully. She reached across the desk to grab his hand, but he rolled the chair backwards out of range and just shook his head.

Tana sagged against the back of her chair, her face instantly flooding with the sadness of shared pain. She didn't know what troubled him, but whatever it was troubled her as well. They were joined together in some strange way she didn't understand, and didn't care if she ever understood. It was enough that the bond was there, making every emotion mutual, all her feelings and responses and thoughts merely reflections of his. In that moment she realised that she had lost a small piece of herself, the piece that would forever be joined to this man, but the loss seemed insignificant.

She heard the faint whistle of a north wind buffeting against the office windows, the distant hum of the generator in the basement, but she was only dimly aware of these things. Even under the mantle of this peculiar, inexplicable sadness, she felt a strange contentment, an extraordinary peace, just to be with him, to have his presence filling her senses.

She saw the dusky gold of the lamplight sprinkled in his hair like fairy-dust from a forgotten childhood tale; she smelled the crisp scent of soap mingled with the fading tang of his aftershave; she heard the tidal sound of his breath, and imagined she could hear the steady, mournful beat of his heart.

Was he as aware of her? she wondered as she rose slowly and circled the desk, stopping when she stood before his chair.

She didn't say anything, and in that moment she wondered what good language was anyway, when it couldn't possibly convey the depth of emotion she was feeling now. Her hands went to his face, and she closed her eyes when her palms closed over the roughness of his jaw, jumped when his hands shot up to cover hers, pressing them hard against his face.

'Tana,' he groaned, reaching for her waist, nearly spanning it with his hands, rising slowly from his chair so that the length of his body brushed against hers. He rested his chin against her forehead briefly, breathing in the clean fragrance of her hair, then he murmured against her brow, 'There's something you have to know.'

No. She raised her eyes to his and shook her head once. No. There was nothing she needed to know. Nothing that words could tell her. Nothing that would make a difference.

'Tana.' He drew her name out into a plea, but she ignored it, reaching up to thread her fingers into his hair, watching the light strands flutter and part, and then close around her hands in a silken caress.

Blue fire flickered in his eyes as he searched hers, his brows tipped in an expression of so many feelings they were beyond isolation and identification. Tana felt the strong hands at her waist tremble, as if they were fighting to jerk her against him and push her away all at the same time. She saw the prominent line of his jaw clenched with effort, the bitter struggle in his eyes, the almost imperceptible flare of his nostrils as his head lowered towards hers, then lifted abruptly away, then lowered helplessly again. She could feel his breath breaking across her nose and cheeks in soft, fragrant puffs of air, syncopation to an unheard rhythm. Suddenly her thighs were against his, denim pressing denim, and then his hands moved with certainty on her waist, pulling her slowly against him until she felt the swollen press of her breasts joining the wall of his chest with a sweet, shattering sensation of pleasure and pain. She pulled helplessly for breath through her open mouth as her eyes fell closed, shuddering at the steaming liquid tide rising within her, and still he denied them both, his mouth hovering just over hers, savouring the anticipation of the inevitable, denying this last, irrevocable, stunning contact while his eyes searched hers.

'This is separate,' he whispered suddenly, his mouth so close that she felt his lips brush against hers when he spoke. 'What happens between us has nothing to do with anything else. None of it is connected. Can you remember that?'

He had her by the shoulders now, and was holding her slightly away, searching her eyes for the answer to a question she couldn't even understand; and it was only because he had increased the distance between them, even slightly, that she heard it at all.

The languorous expression in her half-closed eyes sharpened, and she cocked her head. 'What was that?' she whispered.

He pushed gently at the curtain of hair that swept over her cheek, and tucked it behind her ear. 'I didn't hear anything,' he murmured, winding strands of her hair around his fingers, tugging her head back slightly to lift her face towards his.

She resisted the pressure, her head locking on her neck, her hearing clamouring urgently for attention, demanding that she put aside for a moment the insistent desires of her other senses. 'There was something,' she whispered, her eyes narrowed in uncertainty, and then she heard the sound again and stiffened in his arms. 'There! Did you hear it?'

'No,' he growled impatiently, jerking her against him so strongly that the air left her body in a rush.

'Cody!' she protested in a weak gasp, her forearms straining against his chest, but this time the sound was clearly audible even over the heavy, frantic pulse of his breath, and they both went rigid simultaneously.

'It's Pillar,' she breathed, freezing in his arms for a

moment, then flinging herself away and rushing to the tall windows that faced the yard.

She pressed her fingers against the cold glass until the tips whitened, her eyes straining to see the shed, her heart pounding with the certainty of awful foreboding. Pillar never bawled like that, and the hoarse, shattering trumpet had surely come from the old bull's massive throat. But there was silence now, save for the omnipresent, distant hum of the generator, and the faint whistle of wind beyond the glass. Still, every jangling nerve in her body told her something was wrong, even though the yard lay deep in all its normal night-time shadows, deceptively peaceful.

Her eyes skittered over the landscape, pausing only long enough to identify and discount each familiar object that looked different somehow, shrouded in the cloak of night. Again and again her gaze went back to the loafing shed, looming black and harmless in the distance, melting into its own shadow on the snow whenever a cloud passed over the moon.

Cody had joined her at the window, but she was hardly aware of his presence, her senses were drawn so tight. When he whispered, 'What is it?' she frowned and jerked her head impatiently, her eyes still straining to pierce the darkness.

And then Pillar bawled again, and this time even Cody heard him.

Tana's eyes fixed on the roof of the shed, widened, and then her hand flew to her mouth. 'Dear lord,' she breathed behind her fingers, not even certain that she was speaking aloud. 'Fire.'

Cody's head jerked towards the window, his nose nearly touching the glass, his eyes narrowed, and then he saw the wispy tendril of smoke rising from the shed roof, catching and riding the soft night wind that bent and lifted the slender column until it looked like it was waving a farewell.

In the space of a second he spun towards Tana, his face open with alarm, but she was already gone.

Tana flew through the house on the wings of adrenalin-fuelled panic, mindless of the furious pounding of her heart or the obedient, mechanical responses of her muscles. No process of logic directed her thundering feet to the back entry; no carefully thought-out plan dictated that she snatch her parka on the run, and only pull it on as she was vaulting across the moonlit yard. Consciously thinking of such things would have taken too long, and so her mind and body melded once again into a single unit that operated only on instinct.

She'd heard the heavy pounding of Cody's boots behind her every step of the way, and was relieved to hear him bellow an alarm up the stairs as they rushed past. At least he'd had the presence of mind to alert Zachary and Hazel. She'd forgotten even that.

As her legs pumped furiously through the snow on the way to the shed, her eyes fixed with horror on the rising tendrils of smoke quickening into puffy, ominous billows. And yet, beneath her fear, it was strangely comforting to hear the roar of Cody's laboured breathing just behind her, then beside her, then ahead as his long, powerful legs ate up the ground.

Although the urgent need for speed continued to propel her forwards, the panic inside had quieted slightly to see his coatless form racing past her. Cody was here and, heaven help her, she actually believed that he would somehow save the day, like some improbable cartoon hero. What was it about the man that inspired such blind faith?

When he flung open the door and charged into the shed just ahead of her, she could hear clearly all the cows bawling in terror, smelling the smoke in the loft above their prison, charging and milling and crashing into one another in their panic-stricken attempt to escape.

As Cody looped the end of the watering hose around his shoulders and started to scramble up the ladder towards the smoke-filled loft, Tana rushed blindly through the dark towards the frosty spigot, then cranked it all the way on. She hardly felt the layer of sweat-dampened skin rip from her palm as she jerked it away, then she raced back outside to circuit the building. Without any communication at all, it was understood that Cody's job was to contain the fire, and hers was to open the huge sliding door that would let the cattle escape to the safety of the outside paddock.

Her knees pumping high, trying desperately to run through the enormous drifts of snow piled against the building, Tana fell again and again, but she never felt the frigid trickle of melting snow coursing up her arms and down her neck, never noticed the faint palm prints of blood she left behind whenever she pushed herself up again.

Hurry, hurry, hurry, her mind chanted while frozen clouds of breath exploded from her mouth and the frigid air seared her lungs. In a distant corner of her mind she heard Hazel and Zachary yelling from somewhere between the shed and the house, but she paid no attention. She was nothing more than a machine now, with only one purpose: to get that door opened while the cows still had enough sense to run outside. If the level of their panic became too great, the foolish beasts would be irrevocably locked into the command of their least sensible, yet strongest instinct—to huddle in the one place that had always meant security: the shed that would soon become an oven.

She'd seen it happen before, at Alastair Hunt's barn, when twenty of his best breeding cows jammed themselves into the corner of his flaming calving barn while the door to safety stood wide open. Even as they bellowed in terror, knees buckling as they succumbed to smoke, hair singeing with a sickening smell a twelve-year-old Tana was to remember for the rest of her life, the cows were afraid to leave the place their limited reasoning assumed would always be safe haven, and so they had all died.

'But that won't happen here,' she panted, ducking through the board fence, her hands grasping the side of the huge door at last, her heart and lungs straining as she pushed the monstrous flap of steel along tracks that clattered with ice. 'It won't happen here.'

The cows spilled from the opening in a panicked stampede, bellowing, bucking, dumb with fear, banging against each other in rib-cracking terror as they galloped in ever-widening circles, slipping and crashing on the slick ice of the ploughed paddock, scrambling to their feet again, and finally, numb with exhaustion, settling into a packed huddle of a hundred on the far side of the great fence.

Tana stood off to one side of the door, her mouth open, her shoulders lifting and falling heavily with her laboured breath, thinking that it was a miracle the stupid beasts had had the sense to get out at all. And then Pillar ambled out, turning his great head this way and that as if he were just out for a casual Sunday stroll, and Tana felt weak, relieved laughter rising from her throat as she let her head sag to her chest. It hadn't been a miracle, after all. It was just Pillar, first sounding the alarm, then herding his charges to safety, doing what all bulls instinctively do best.

'Good boy,' she exhaled, shaking her head in wonder when the old bull strode casually up to her and, with a butt that was gentle for him, nearly knocked her down. She fumbled in her pocket for a cube of sugar, offered it on her bloody palm, then winced when the big tongue swiped it clean.

Suddenly her head jerked upwards, remembering, and she scrambled away from the indignant bull, back around the side of the building towards the door to the loft. Hazel was standing at the entrance, her head laid back on her shoulders to look up at the roof, hugging her arms to her chest and stamping her feet. Her head dropped and spun when she heard Tana's weak call.

'It's out!' she bellowed across the snow, seeing Tana's frantic stumbling through the deep snow. 'Take it easy! The fire's out! We just lost a few bales of hay, that's all!'

They were all slumped in various postures of exhaustion around the kitchen table, except for Hazel, who was bustling about in her old brown terry robe, making coffee, heating soup, slicing home-made bread. She looked younger somehow, with the heavy coil of her braid looped over her shoulder instead of pinned on top of her head. A few sleep-mussed wisps of greying brown curled over her broad brow, gentling the width of her face, making her look almost girlish.

'Well,' she grumbled importantly, pausing in her

work to jam her fists into her ample hips as she shook her head at the slouched threesome, 'I just shudder to think what the bathtubs in this house are going to look like when you three get finished with them.'

Tana smiled tiredly, glancing around the table. Zach looked as though the black of his hair had leaked down over his face, leaving streaks of dark soot that matched his eyes—eyes that looked strangely happy, now that she thought about it, but why not? They all had reason to be happy. Not one head lost or even injured, and all but a few bales of hay saved.

Her glance drifted to Cody, and her eyes softened. He'd handled the worst of the fire before Zach had arrived to help, and still wore the evidence of his labours. That glorious light hair was streaked with caked soot, clinging to the sides of his head, spiked erratically on the crown where he had pushed it back with his fingers. Beneath a fine layer of grey ash, his face was pink with what looked like the beginnings of a sunburn, and the beautiful eyes were reddened and watery from smoke.

'You sure you're all right?' she asked solicitously when he coughed, and the brilliant white flash of a reassuring smile split the shadow on his jaw.

'We did all right, you and I,' he murmured, giving voice to the extraordinary sense of partnership between them, reinforcing that feeling by reaching over to touch her tenderly on the cheek.

As soon as he touched her all her senses circled around the space that contained the two of them, weaving an invisible, invincible cocoon that shut out Zach and Hazel and everything else in the world.

She felt her eyes link with his, felt his warmth flowing

to her and then back to him and then back to her again, until she couldn't be sure where it had all begun, only that it was an endless circle that bound them together as surely as the singleness of purpose that had first sent them racing together towards the loafing shed, then on to perform their individual tasks without a word passing between them, as if communication had already taken place on a much deeper level.

At some point in that breathless run, or perhaps it had happened long before that, Tana had felt the complete and utter joy of spiritual union; she had become part of something greater than herself, something that banished forever that awful sense of solitude that lives on in any relationship that doesn't touch the soul.

'Yes,' she answered him with a smiling sigh that crossed the space between them with the softness of a summer breeze. 'We did all right.'

Instinct, she thought wryly, not caring any more what kind of a name you put to whatever drew them together.

'How touching.' The harsh, metallic rasp of Zach's sarcasm shattered the protective cocoon. Tana frowned uncertainly, then her eyes cleared and focused on Zach's dark countenance. Had she been a little more alert at that moment, she would have been frightened by the malicious gleam in the black eyes that watched her. 'He's played you for a fool, Tana,' he drawled, dark brows winging over even darker eyes. 'He's played you for a fool from day one, and tonight he almost won the game. You're sitting next to the man who tried to burn down the barn and kill those precious cows of yours.'

For a breath of time the kitchen went deadly silent, and Tana just sat there, staring at Zach in utter disbelief, so stunned by his preposterous accusation that she was incapable of responding to it. Dimly, as if she were watching and listening from a great distance, she heard Hazel breathe, 'What?' and saw Cody shoot straight up from his chair into a rigid tower of quivering rage.

She lifted her eyes slowly to Cody's face, absolutely powerless to move, mystified by this sudden inexplicable turn of events. Hazel, fortunately, was too practical to be paralysed, and jumped between the two men, pressing her broad back against Cody with her arms spread as if Zach intended to attack, when clearly it was the other way around. Zach remained seated, even going so far as to lean back in his chair and grin slyly at Cody's furious countenance, straining over Hazel's shoulder as if she had suddenly sprouted a second head.

'You son of a bitch,' Cody hissed, his face white beneath the layer of soot, his hands reaching for Hazel's shoulders to shove her aside.

It was something about his hands and arms, so tense that muscle and sinew bulged and rippled under the blackened skin, that brought Tana suddenly to life. Hazel had been right, after all. They were going to kill each other.

'Zach!' she shouted, leaping to her feet, leaning across the table until the still-damp mass of her hair hung like wrinkled curtains on either side of her face. 'What are you saying? Are you crazy? Why would Cody try to burn down the barn?'

Zachary savoured the drama of a pause before replying, looking straight at her. 'Because,' he said finally, 'if Pillar and those cows live, D.C. Enterprises won't be able to foreclose on this place.' He took a deep, satisfying breath, then continued with a smile that chilled Tana to the bone, 'and Douglas Cody *is* D.C. Enterprises. That was his office that called, not the phone company. They were looking for their president, the man who came here before the storm to personally serve you with the foreclosure papers.' He turned his head to look at Cody. 'Your friends were worried about you, Douglas, not hearing from you in so long. I took the liberty of telling them you were just fine, and they were as pleased as they could be. Said they'd send a helicopter for you tomorrow morning. I assured them you'd be ready and waiting.'

Tana was still leaning over the table, her face frozen into a white, expressionless tableau. Her eyes looked strangely pale, as if their normal rich brown colour had been suddenly drained away, and though they were fixed on Zach's face she didn't really see him at all.

It was impossible for her mind to absorb the enormity of what Zach had said, and so for the moment it ignored the bulk of it, and concentrated on the accusation of arson, the only thing she could deal with at the time.

'Cody was with me.' Her lips formed the words like a memorised lesson. 'He was with me when the fire started. We saw it together.'

Zach peered over the steeple of his fingers, and although his expression was blank, it gave the impression of a suppressed laugh. 'Really? Were you together when the fire started—when the fire was *set*? Or just when you noticed it for the first time?'

Tana's eyes remained quiet while her mind roared behind them, trying to pull detail from memory. Cody . . . alone downstairs while the rest of them sought sleep . . . downstairs? Or outside? Could he have just come in when she found him? He hadn't heard that first noise . . . or perhaps he had *pretended* not to hear it . . . tried to distract her by . . .

She closed her eyes briefly and saw an image of the tall, blond horseman riding up the mountain, his hat dusted with the first flakes of snow; then the image blurred and shifted and he was riding Mac next to the thundering herd, lasso at the ready, face young and joyous and fulfilled; and then he was outside, staring up at the stars as if he owned them all. No. That man loved this life, this country, this place. He could never wantonly, willingly destroy it. Unless—a nasty little voice told her—unless he wanted it for his own, and that was the only way to get it.

The heavy weight of unbearable despair hit the bottom of her stomach like a rock, and she wondered why it was that her body remained together in one piece, while inside she was falling apart into a million irreconcilable fragments.

She felt like a dead thing, an empty shell that only resembled a living person, as she straightened slowly, almost painfully, and turned her head to meet Cody's eyes. Save for a few smudges of soot acquired when she insisted on checking for herself that the fire was out, there was no colour at all in her face. The full, unkempt tangle of her black hair framed an oval of ghastly white. Only the quiet, mournful plea of her eyes indicated life. 'Is it true?' she whispered, locking her watery knees so she could stay upright. Deny it! she was screaming in her head. Deny it all, damn you! But her voice was quiet when she went on. 'Is D.C. Enterprises your company? Is that really why you came here in the first place? To serve the foreclosure papers?'

All the rage drained from Cody's face as he looked at her, leaving a blank space that told her nothing. 'Yes. That much is true.'

To Tana's credit, her shoulders slumped only slightly, almost imperceptibly, and she nodded vacantly, as if that was the answer she'd expected all along. 'I see,' she said in a flat, lifeless voice. 'No wonder you hadn't planned on spending the winter. You weren't a bed-and-board hand after all, but once you were stuck here, telling us the truth . . .' she shook her head with a sick smile, 'that would have been very awkward, wouldn't it?'

At this, Cody's mouth twitched slightly, as if he would smile, but all he did was nod once.

Tana felt a prolonged, painful sigh rise in her chest as she glanced around the room with eyes that saw nothing. For the moment, she had no sense of where she was, or what she was doing there.

'Tana.' He spoke sharply, and when she turned to look at him she saw the first hint of animation in his face. She waited, her expression placid and empty.

'Think about it, Tana,' he hissed desperately. 'For goodness' sake, think about it for a minute. Ask yourself why . . .'

'Oh, I will,' she interrupted him with the strangest smile, suddenly feeling the presence of her legs as they carried her away from the table towards the hall . . .

'Tana, wait! Let me explain!'

Her feet hesitated for just an instant, responding to his voice even when her mind wouldn't. Instinct again. She almost laughed out loud, but instead she lifted her chin and began the endless walk down the hall towards the stairs, slamming the door on her senses until she heard nothing of the clattering ruckus that errupted behind her.

CHAPTER THIRTEEN

TANA sat behind her father's desk, her head propped wearily in one hand while her other pencilled notes on a piece of paper already cluttered with figures. Broad bars of sunlight from the oversized windows warmed the room, striping the wood floor with bands of yellow. One such band crossed Tana's head, making the full crown of dark hair sparkle with life.

And that's the only sign of life in her, Hazel thought grumpily, glancing up from her knitting as if to reassure herself that Tana was still in the room at all. The slender woman behind the desk looked something like the old Tana, but not much. There was no softness in this woman's face: no trust, no vulnerability, no chinks in this new armour of coldness. She had wrapped herself in a cloak of determination never to be betrayed again, but it had sapped the warmth from her voice and her presence, and sometimes Hazel felt chilled just being in the same room with her.

She eyed Tana critically, shaking her big head in silent exasperation. She'd grown thinner in the last four weeks—ever since that awful noisy whirlybird had landed in the front yard and whisked Douglas Cody back to Dallas and out of their lives—and Hazel didn't care how many times Tana protested that she was absolutely, perfectly fine and to leave her alone—she *wasn't* fine, and it was beginning to look as if she'd never be fine again.

Her face was pale and drawn, with faint shadows beneath the large, dark eyes, and even her body looked fragile beneath the heavy, dark sweaters she had taken to wearing over her jeans. For all the chill of her emotionless demeanour, for all her pretence of apathy, there were still times when Hazel caught a glimpse of the layer beneath—the terrible, empty despair of the walking wounded—and those times made her want to cry and swear all at the same time.

Cody could fix that, damn his hide, if he'd just come back and set things right. He'd said he was going to, and without a single good reason to believe him Hazel had anyway, fool that she was.

'I've got to talk to her, Hazel,' he'd told her the morning after Zach had gleefully dropped his bombshell. 'But she's locked the door to her room, won't even answer when I knock. I didn't start that fire, Hazel. Surely you believe that.'

And Hazel had. Barn fires could start a hundred different ways. Spontaneous combustion of a heated, mouldering bale of hay, electrical sparks, lots of things. Not that she had proof of that, but, just looking at Cody's devastated face that morning, she'd known in her bones that he was telling the truth. Of course, she couldn't tell Tana that. Tana wouldn't listen to a single sentence that began with the man's name.

'Some day I'll have the proof, Hazel,' he'd said then, 'and then I'll be back.'

But that had been four long weeks ago, and the promise was beginning to wear thin.

She sighed heavily and leaned over the desk. 'How's it look, Tana?'

The soft fluff of sunlit black shifted as Tana lifted her head and blinked at Hazel. She was still beautiful, almost achingly beautiful, Hazel thought, but it was the two-dimensional beauty of a lifeless statue of cold stone.

'See for yourself.' Tana spun the paper across the desk. 'If half those cows deliver, we'll make more than enough at the breeding auction to build up the herd again.'

Hazel peered at the figures, then nodded with satisfaction. '*And* pay off the mortgage,' she added.

Tana smiled at her, but the smile was empty.

Hazel watched her face carefully, waiting for any indication of emotion, no matter how slight, but there was none. 'That's good news, Tana. You should be at least a little bit pleased.'

Tana just continued to smile vacantly, and Hazel's knitting needles clattered with impatience. She pursed her lips and forced a steady quiet into her voice. 'Tana,' she said firmly, 'in all our years together, we've talked about everything. Everything, good and bad. I know how badly you've been hurt, but I just can't stand the silence that's grown up between us. It has to stop. We have to talk about it. About Cody. It's time, child.' This last was said so kindly that Tana bit down on her usual, snappish retort whenever Cody's name was mentioned.

Her mouth opened as if to speak, then closed again. There was the slight squeak of a floorboard expanding with the heat of the sun, but other than that the office was perfectly still.

'You know damn well he didn't start that fire, Tana. In your heart, you know he wasn't that kind of a man . . .'

Tana interrupted quietly, looking Hazel right in the

eye. 'He wanted the ranch, Hazel. That's why he came in the first place. You keep forgetting that.'

'I'm not forgetting that, dammit! But if that was what he really wanted, why the hell did he help you bring those cattle down? Why did he do the one thing that would guarantee you *wouldn't* lose the place? Why didn't he just slap that paper in your hand up on the mountain and ride away? Just tell me that!' Her face was flushed with emotion, her eyes bright.

Tana shook her head sadly, and Hazel realised suddenly that her smile wasn't empty; it was full of sympathy. 'Poor Hazel,' she murmured. 'You don't understand. The minute Douglas Cody set foot inside the front door, bringing the cows down ceased to matter.'

Hazel's eyes sharpened warily. 'What's that supposed to mean?'

Tana closed her eyes and let a long sigh escape from her pursed lips. 'I called the courthouse the day he left, when I found this . . .' she picked up a legal-looking document from the desk and waved it in the air '. . . tucked inside the ledgers where he left it. It's the announcement of foreclosure, Hazel, and as long as it was delivered *before* we paid off the mortgage, there was no way to stop the proceedings.' Her lips lifted in a bitter smile. 'As I said, Hazel—the minute he walked in the front door. That's when we lost Mitchell Ranch. It isn't ours any more.'

There was a soft, unnoticed clatter as Hazel's knitting needles hit the floor.

'I know he didn't set the fire,' Tana went on dully. 'No reason for him to do that. The ranch was already his, no matter how much money we made at the spring auction, and he knew it. All that time he was with us, pretending to be part of us, part of this place . . .'

She caught her breath at the sight of Hazel's face, suddenly sagging with the dull, heartbreaking astonishment of one who has just seen hope fragmented and tossed aside.

'Oh, Hazel,' she murmured, rushing around the desk to wrap her arms around the older woman, cursing herself for not understanding that she would not be the only one hurt by Cody's betrayal. 'Hazel, I'm sorry,' she whispered into the older woman's neck. 'I'm so sorry.' For the first time she understood that, in her own way, Hazel had loved Douglas Cody too; and, worse yet, had trusted him.

'Did you tell Zach?' Hazel asked brokenly.

'Yes. He was with me when I found the papers, and when I called the courthouse.' Tana felt the awkward pat of a large hand on her back, and remembered rocking in these very arms a hundred times as a child, finding comfort there. 'It's going to be all right, Hazel.' Her eyes glistened with tears she refused to let fall. 'Zach still has his land, and that's where we'll live. We'll still have a place; it just won't be this one.'

'No!' Hazel gritted, pushing Tana away by the shoulders, her eyes dark and her brow furrowed. 'No, Tana. Not that way . . .'

'Tana?' Zach's rich baritone crossed the room from the doorway, and Tana straightened quickly, composing her features. Out of the corner of her eye, she saw Hazel brush hastily at her eyes, then rise from her chair and leave the room by the other door.

'Hello, Zach. Finished outside already?'

Zach stood uncertainly in the doorway, twisting his hat in his hands, and Tana thought she saw compassion in his face, and loved him for that, at least. 'Hazel OK?' he asked quietly.

'She's fine.' Tana stood in smiling immobility as he crossed the room, quelling the impulse to turn and run from him, just so she wouldn't have to face the inevitable. She would marry Zach when he asked. There weren't any other choices left. She knew it, and he knew it, but she didn't think she could bear to hear it confirmed aloud. Not just yet.

He tossed his hat on a chair, then took her gently by the shoulders and bent his handsome head to kiss her cheek. She submitted docilely, wondering why his lips always felt so cold.

'It's time we talked about the future, Tana. About us,' he said softly.

She tried to smile, but it felt as if his fingers were pressing deep into the flesh of her shoulders, even though she knew they were only resting there lightly. She looked up into his eyes briefly, then had to turn her head away.

He captured her chin between thumb and forefinger and tipped it gently upward. 'What is it, Tana? Is it me?'

She shook her head slightly, looking down. 'It's not you, Zach. You've been wonderful. It's just . . .' She shrugged helplessly and his eyes hardened.

'Cody.' He spit out the word with loathing, jerking his hands away, spinning to pace back and forth in front of the desk. Tana followed him with her eyes, almost impersonally.

Poor Zach. He'd tried so hard, and he *had* been wonderful, treading so carefully over her fractured feelings this past month, staying quietly in the background, giving her the time and space she needed to assess the past and evaluate the future. He had kept every conversation light, never until this moment so much as mentioning Cody's name, never pressuring her, never forcing himself into her awareness, just waiting patiently, silently, for the response she hadn't been able to give him. He deserved better.

She smiled as she watched the barely contained, frustrated energy of his pacing. His jeans whistled as his long, muscular legs scissored across the floor, a dark thatch of hair springing from his brow, and those angry, mysterious eyes reflecting the burning impatience of a man better suited to action than to words. For the first time in a long time, she openly acknowledged the fact that, objectively speaking, Zachary Chase was every bit as appealing as he had always been. He was still the tall, ruggedly handsome cowboy of her youthful dreams—powerful, commanding, relentlessly masculine—and if she still found something about him vaguely disturbing, that was only an instinctive reaction, not a realistic one, and heaven knew her instincts hadn't been very reliable up to this point. Hadn't it been instinct that had sucked her into the web of Cody's deceit, and hadn't it been Zach who had finally proven how traitorous that instinct had been?

As if he had heard her thoughts, he stopped suddenly in his pacing and touched her with his eyes, and she felt herself swimming, then sinking into those black, bottomless depths.

He was on her in such a rush that he took her breath away, his mouth travelling hungrily up the side of her neck, one hand twisting her hair into tangles while the other clutched at her back, and, with a distance that seemed positively amazing under the circumstances, she wondered what he had seen in her face that had spurred him into action. Suddenly he grabbed her hips and jerked her urgently against him, and as she fought for just one gasp of air all the vague uneasiness she had felt about Zach for all these years began to gel into a fuzzy alignment she thought might become clear, if she could just concentrate on it for a moment.

'Zach, wait,' she complained, pushing flat-handed against his chest while she twisted her head to the side.

'I've waited for nine years,' he said hoarsely, his breathing hot and ragged upon her face. 'That's long enough.'

Suddenly Tana sensed an edge to his masculinity; a sharp, slashing edge that demanded control—whether it be horse or machine or woman—and she shuddered once, then pushed so strongly against him that he took two stumbling steps backwards, his arms flailing, his mouth open in surprise.

Breathing heavily, she faced him with her head down, her lips compressed, her shoulders hunched against the explosion of rage she expected from him. To her surprise he just tipped his head back and laughed. It wasn't the laugh of a man chagrined by loss; it was the dark, mirthless laughter of a man who knew that ultimately he would win, and the sound sent shivers up her spine. She heard the blood rushing in her ears, the steady thump of her heart, growing louder and louder— impossibly loud, as if her heart were an airborne thing, an immense, mechanical pump descending on the house—and then suddenly she realised that the deafening thumping wasn't the beat of her heart at all.

Hazel appeared in the doorway, her expression calm, her hands busy with dishtowel and dripping glass. 'It's a helicopter,' she said, with no more emotion than if she had announced dinner. 'Cody's back.'

Cody's back—the words reverberated in Tana's skull, setting up a chain reaction of quicksilver feelings she kept from showing on her face because Zach and Hazel were both watching her. Logically, she knew there was only one reason for Douglas Cody's return—he intended to take possession of what was now his ranch. Knowing that, she should have felt trepidation, indignation, or at the very least anxiety; but these were not the emotions she was barely managing to contain. At the moment, the only feeling she could identify was anticipation.

Cody's back, and that means something is going to happen, she told herself; but her mind stumbled and stopped on the first two words of that thought, because they were the only important ones.

If her pride had permitted it, she would have cried aloud then, because it was first time she truly understood that there was bondage in bonding; that Cody's hold on her transcended the rational, carrying her along like a helpless passenger on a storm-tossed boat. He had deceived her, betrayed her, taken her home and her heart, and still the most important thing in the world at this moment was simply that he was here, that she would look on his face again.

She chastised herself silently, bitterly, as she led the way to the large front hall. By all rights she should be facing the door with a gun, waiting for Cody's entrance, but instead she had to grit her teeth to keep the joy from her face. You're disgusting, she told herself: mindless, weak, and unforgivably stupid. With an enormous effort of will, she dredged up the last vestiges of her pride to keep her features stiff, never realising that what she really felt shone clearly in her eyes.

The three of them assembled solemnly in the entry-way. Tana was the spearhead of the trio, standing slighly ahead and apart, looking poignantly valiant with her chin lifted stubbornly, her hair tumbling back over her shoulders like a centurion's cape, her eyes focused steadily on the huge front door. She seemed lost in the bulk of her black sweater, smaller than she really was, but the aura of her control was almost visible, and for the first time in weeks she exuded vitality. Hazel, standing back a step to her left, was proud of her.

Zachary loomed like a malevolent spirit behind Tana and to the right, his eyes narrowed with suspicion, his jaw set, every muscle in his body clearly tensed and ready to spring. He looked more like a formless black presence than a man, and there was a vicious alertness to his posture that reminded Hazel of a bull's ominous stance when he perceived a threat to his herd.

They all listened to the dull whumping of the chopper's rotors slicing through the winter air just outside the door, and then the sound slowed, and stopped.

There was a brief, hard knock at the door before it was flung open to thump against the rubber stopper on the wall. Cody stood framed in the white backlight of a winter landscape.

Even as Tana straightened slightly, lifting her chin even higher, she felt herself crumble inside, because, whatever else Douglas Cody was, he was also incredibly beautiful at this moment. He stood in the doorway in a one-piece white ski-suit, hair lifting from his head in a blond wave, looking more like an avenging angel than the villain he was supposed to be. His eyes were sparks of blue light in the golden shadows of his face, and they crackled across the empty space towards her, flickering slightly in the only greeting that mattered.

Tana's face went even more rigid, but her eyes met his in a hot, liquid gaze that stripped away her expressionless mask, and showed Cody the truth of what was beneath.

His lips curved upwards at the sight, then parted in a wide, white, glorious smile. 'I'm back,' he said quietly, and the words were meant only for her, because there was no one else there.

Suddenly Tana felt the rough grasp of Zach's hand on her waist, and she blinked in surprise as he pulled her against him possissively.

'We can see that,' he said snidely, turning slightly to place himself between Tana and Cody. 'The question is, why? There's nothing here for you.'

Cody's smile faded and softened, but his eyes remained fixed on Tana. 'You're wrong about that,' he said quietly, and Tana felt the tug of his words and his gaze even more strongly than the sudden jerk of Zach pulling her even closer.

'The hell I am. This place may belong to you eventually, but not until the foreclosure is finalised. In the meantime, you've got no business here, and in case you haven't guessed, you're not welcome. Now, get the hell out of my house.'

Tana was so preoccupied with the way Cody was looking at her that she heard Zach's voice only dimly, but there had been something wrong with what he said. Her brows twitched slightly.

'Your house?' Cody tore his gaze from Tana with obvious reluctance, and arched one brow at Zachary.

'This has never been your house, and it never will be.' His mouth twitched in a smile. 'And the foreclosure was finalised yesterday. I've brought the papers with me.'

Tana, still trapped in the vice of Zachary's arm, felt her stomach lurch. 'So soon?' she whispered.

'It doesn't matter, Tana,' Zach said gruffly, still glaring at Cody. 'We've still got the cattle. We'll start building a house on my land, just as soon as we get married.'

'You don't own any land.'

Tana felt the convulsive jerk of Zachary's hand, and sensed his entire body stiffening next to her. 'What are you talking about, Cody?' she asked, confused. 'Zachary owns a lot of land.'

Cody's eyes shifted to her and softened. 'No. *You* own a lot of land, Tana. Since he bought it with your father's money, it belongs to you now.'

She'd heard the words; it was just that they didn't make any sense. 'My father's money . . .?' she echoed weakly, not understanding, her gaze darting from Cody's grim expression to Hazel's wide-eyed astonishment, and then finally, when she had the courage, to Zach.

At first his countenance appeared frozen, absolutely unyielding; but then, as she watched, his features seemed to sag like a melting mask of hot wax. She heard a weak, incredulous voice, and it took a moment before she realised it was her own.

'That can't be true,' she mumbled. Her lips felt thick, numb, barely able to form words. 'Tell him, Zach. Tell him it isn't true.'

Cody looked at her and sighed, his lips tightened in sympathy. There was no trace of smugness, no satisfaction in his voice when he finally spoke. 'But it is true,

Tana. I'm sorry.'

'No.' She kept shaking her head, refusing to believe it even when she felt Zach's arm drop away from her waist. 'Tell him, Zach. Tell him he's wrong!' she begged him, but Zachary only closed his eyes and turned his head away.

'Zachary?' Tana whispered, reaching tentatively for his arm, jumping when he jerked it away and turned his back.

Cody was talking now, saying things that were probably important, and she turned to look up at him as if that would help the words sink into a mind that didn't want to hear.

'You had plenty of good grazing during the drought, Tana, and you didn't lose any cattle to disease, either. Zach sold them off and kept the money, just as he kept all the money he said went to buy supplemental feed. Actually, it went to buy land. Lots of it. All in his name.'

The hall was strangely silent, and somehow that didn't seem right. Revelations like this should be accompanied by an explosion of noise that assaulted the eardrums as mercilessly as the truth was assaulting her mind. There should be motion, too; confusion. Zachary should be launching himself towards Cody at this moment, shouting denials, striking out at the man who dared level such an accusation. But he wasn't.

It was true. Even if she'd been able to ignore Cody's words, to rationalise them away somehow, Zachary was admitting his guilt by saying nothing, but just standing there like a frozen frame in a home movie.

Mindlessly, her eyes wide and glazed, Tana sidestepped away from Zachary and into Hazel's big arms, because there was no comfort anywhere else in the world any more, and perhaps there never had been. She had been betrayed by the man she loved, and then betrayed again by the man she thought she could learn to love, and the world was suddenly a barren, empty place with only this one safe harbour.

'Why, Zach?' she whispered, and for the first time Zachary turned his head and looked at her, and she saw clearly in his eyes what she had never wanted to see before.

'Why not?' he said bitterly. 'It should have been mine, anyway. The ranch, the cattle, you . . . all of it should have been mine. And it would have been, if you hadn't run away that first time. You should have stayed, Tana. You should have stayed and married me, and none of this would have happened.' He turned away again and shrugged. 'I knew you'd come back to the land eventually, and when your dad got laid up, I saw my chance to make sure you came back to me, too. If you lost this place, you'd have had to come to mine.'

He met her eyes briefly, and suddenly Tana saw that he wasn't sorry for what he had done; he was only sorry he'd been caught.

She closed her eyes to the sight of him and waited for the onslaught of feeling, waited to be overpowered by despair, but all she felt was a sick emptiness, as if she had been robbed of the capacity to feel at all.

'And that's why he tried to burn the loafing shed,' Cody added flatly.

'What?' Tana gasped, her eyes flying open in horror.

'He didn't know then that the foreclosure was inevitable, Tana. He thought you could still save the place by selling the spring calves, so he had to make sure they were never born.'

In her mind Tana flew across the room and attacked the man she had trusted for as long as she could remember, a man so cold that he could crush the dreams of others to attain his own; but in reality all she did was stand there, staring at Zachary with a bleak indifference that masked her thoughts.

She was only dimly aware of the front door opening, of two deputies entering with quiet deference, as if someone in the family had just died. She didn't say a word as they grasped Zach's elbows and led him outside to the waiting helicopter. At the last moment Zachary looked over his shoulder at her, the icy wind whipping his black hair across his brow. Cody closed the door quietly, blocking off the view of the helicopter rising away.

'Will he go to gaol?' she asked tonelessly.

'Don't even think about that now.' Hazel gave her shoulders a quick squeeze and then led her into the living-room and settled her into a chair. Tana was barely aware of crossing the floor, of lowering herself carefully into the chair like an old woman whose brittle bones might shatter at any moment. It wasn't the end of the world, she was telling herself. Finding out that a man she had trusted for years had betrayed her wasn't the end of the world. It could have been worse. She could have married him. She closed her eyes and shuddered at the thought. At least Cody had saved her from that.

'I think we could all use some brandy, Hazel,' Cody said quietly, kneeling in front of Tana, taking her hands gently in his. Hazel nodded and disappeared into the kitchen.

Tana looked down at his hands without really seeing them.

'I know it was a shock,' he said quietly, 'and I'm sorry

the truth had to hurt you so much, but it had to be told. You had to know.'

She smiled a little, looking past his shoulder across the room. The hurt hadn't really sunk in yet, not all the way; but even when it did she'd be able to take it. She still had the cattle, and now she had land of her own, and any Mitchell could build a life with that. 'I think I knew it all the time,' she murmured, staring off across the room, remembering that strange foreboding that had made her reject Zach the first time, in spite of his appeal. 'Whenever I thought about it rationally, I couldn't think of a single reason not to marry Zach. And yet, as kind as he was, as loyal as he was, there was always something . . .' she paused and frowned '. . . some feeling I had that I couldn't quite put my finger on . . .'

'Instinct?'

'Instinct,' she repeated, nodding slowly, still looking off into the distance. 'Yes, I suppose that's what it was.'

For a moment she felt as if she had gone somewhere far away, somewhere deep inside herself where no one else could follow. It was a safe place—no one could hurt her here—but it was a lonely place, too.

'Tana.'

It took an enormous effort for Tana to shift her eyes to meet his.

'What did your instincts tell you about me?' His gaze was earnest, almost fearful.

Even though it seemed ridiculous now, truth was truth, and it wasn't as hard to say it aloud as she thought it would be. 'To trust you,' she said softly. 'I told you that the very first day we met, remember?' She shook her head at the memory, finally seeing the irony. 'My goodness, you must have been laughing at me then. You were the

villain, weren't you? The wicked lien holder coming to
take away my ranch, and I trusted you.'

'I never laughed,' he said quietly, then he pulled her to
her feet. 'Come with me. I have something to show you.'

Hazel was just gathering brandy and glasses on to a tray
when they entered the kitchen doorway. 'Sit down,
Hazel,' Cody told her. 'I have a story to tell, and you
should hear it too. Do you see this, Tana?' He pointed at
a series of jagged lines cut into the wooden frame of the
door.

'My growth chart,' Tana nodded with a small smile.
'Once a year when I was a kid I'd stand here, and my dad
would carve a mark in the wood to show . . .'

'Right. And this?' He turned her gently by the
shoulders to face the other side of the doorframe and
pointed to a similar row of carved lines.

'Another kid's chart. We figured it was from the family
that lived here before we did.'

'And this?' Cody dropped to his knees, pulling her
down with him, and pointed to a faint carving on the
wood near the floor.

Tana crouched close, frowning at the barely visible
scars in the wood. 'I never noticed that before. Looks like
initials . . .' She stilled suddenly, her eyes fixed.

'Right again,' Cody said quietly. 'D.C. Douglas Cody.'
He rose wearily to his feet, then leaned back against the
frame as if he would now measure how much he had
grown since the last line had been carved so many years
before.

Tana rose opposite him, sagging back against her own
chart, not realising that they were facing each other now
as the reminders of their youth had faced each other for
years. 'You grew up in this house?' she asked in a small

voice.

One side of his mouth lifted in a wry smile. 'I told you we were so much alike you wouldn't believe it, remember? I was just about eight years ahead of you, that's all. I was sixteen when my parents were killed, when I left here. Shortly after that, your family moved in.'

Tana just stared at him, her mouth slightly open.

'I ran from this place, just as you did later. Used your dad's down-payment on the ranch to invest in some oil options, and that was the beginning of D.C. Enterprises. Within a few years, I had just about everything that money could buy, but somehow it wasn't enough. Something was missing, and I finally figured out what it was.' He sighed, remembering the years of obsessive longing for this one house, this one piece of ground. 'I'd sold my heritage, my roots, and there was no way to get it back . . . until your dad started missing payments and opened the door for repossession.'

Tana couldn't stop nodding as she began to understand one thing after another. Dear heaven, no wonder she had felt such a strong link to this man; no wonder she had sensed that they were rediscovering the land together, that they both belonged here; that their lives were somehow intertwined . . .

'I know the rest,' she whispered, but Cody stopped her with a hand under her chin, tipping her face up until he could see her eyes.

'No, Tana, you don't know the rest.' His eyes shifted from hers to watch his fingers thread through her hair, smoothing it away from her face. It never occurred to her to pull away from the touch of his hand. 'I came here to offer to buy you out. I still had the foreclosure notice if you refused, but I never expected that you would. My investigators told me that you hadn't lived here in years; that you had no interest in the ranch whatsoever; that you'd jump at the chance to sell.' His lips compressed and his head moved from side to side in bafflement. 'And then we met up on the mountain, and in spite of everything I'd heard, you were fighting for your home just as I was fighting for mine, and the terrible, sick irony of it was that we were fighting for the same home, for the same reasons. I never meant to deceive you, Tana. It just . . . happened.'

Tana reached up, removed his hand from her hair and placed it gently at his side, tempering the gesture with a sad smile. For some reason, she couldn't talk when he was touching her.

'Well,' she said with forced lightness, 'at least we're both back where we belong now, and if I really own all that land Zach bought, we'll be neighbours, won't we?' She almost laughed aloud at the irony.

'Neighbours? Neighbours?' he repeated, his brows furrowed. 'What are you talking about?'

Tana closed her eyes, tried to hate him for snatching away her home just when she'd rediscovered it, but failed. It was his home too, after all, and who could better understand how much that meant? It would be difficult, of course, living near him, bumping into him in town, forever an outsider to the life he would make here, the family he would start . . . she winced at the thought of another woman living in this house with him, loving him, having his children . . . She swallowed the lump in her throat and spoke brightly. 'We won't be able to start a house on the new land until spring, of course, so I'm afraid we'll have to ask you for a little more time . . .'

'What? Time for what?'

She looked up at him, her dark eyes wide and puzzled. 'To vacate your property, of course.'

She was certain he'd been standing perfectly straight, but that couldn't be, because now he seemed to be growing taller and taller as she watched, shooting up another inch for every shade his face darkened.

'You think I went through all this so we could be neighbours?' he shouted. The sheer volume of his voice forced her back even tighter against the doorframe as she stared up at him, completely mystified. 'Is *that* what your instincts tell you? And do you think I'm fool enough to make the same mistake twice? To walk away without a fight from what really matters, for the second time in my life?'

Tana just stared at him, trying to absorb what he said, trying to make sense of it.

Suddenly his whole body dropped in utter exasperation. 'For goodness' sake, Tana, don't tell me you don't feel what I do. Don't tell me you think this could have ended any other way. This isn't *my* property! It's *ours*. It always has been, really, only now it's legal. The new deed is in both our names.'

Tana's lips opened to ask why he had done such a thing, and then froze in place because she didn't have to ask. She knew.

Ours, her mind murmured over and over again as she looked at him, feeling her eyes fill and not caring. She heard a soft sniffle in the background, and remembered Hazel's presence for the first time in a long time, and then forgot it again when Cody cupped her face in both hands and smiled down at her so tenderly that she thought her heart would break just looking at him.

His eyes seemed to deepen, pulling her into the blue

depths that didn't reflect her image as much as they seemed to absorb it. The warmth of his low chuckle filled her senses. 'You and I, Tana,' he whispered. 'Part of each other from the beginning; one life reflecting the other long before we even met. We belong together, as much as we belong here.'

She felt it again—that same, deep sense of oneness she had felt with him so often, and only with him. It was an almost indestructible sense of union, and now she realised that it had always been there, that it had been the prelude to desire, that the desire itself was merely the physical manifesation of something much greater, something very real, yet so elusive, so complex, that man had never been able to describe it properly, and so he called it instinct.

'You love me,' she said simply, but there was wonder in her eyes.

'And you love me,' he replied.

Hazel, watching and listening in quiet, teary-eyed attention from her seat at the kitchen table, startled them both when she jerked a handkerchief from her apron pocket and blew her nose noisily. 'Well,' she said gruffly, trying for a stern expression and failing miserably, 'what happens now?'

'The obvious,' Cody smiled down at Tana's glowing face. 'Three for supper, Hazel. From now on.'

Hazel crossed her arms under her breasts and scowled and beamed all at the same time. 'Won't look good,' she said decisively. 'Man shouldn't live in the same house with two women without marrying one of them.'

'My sentiments exactly,' he agreed, then lifted his shoulders in an elaborate shrug. 'But which one?'

CHAPTER FOURTEEN

THERE was a crispness to the air that night that Tana could never remember noticing before, a clarity to the thousands of stars that winked in the soaring canopy of black. And, over the crunch of their boots in the snow, a deep, peaceful silence blanketed the land.

She felt Cody's hand squeeze hers under the double layers of their gloves, and looked over at him and smiled. There was moonlight in his hair and on his face, and she caught her breath at the wonder of it.

He stopped suddenly and put his arm around her, turning her gently until the ranch buildings were at their backs, and they faced the dark pyramids of the shadowy mountains looming just ahead. The moon danced on the snowy peaks, making it look as if the land itself wore crowns of light, and Tana trembled with the sense of something far more profound than a man and a woman walking in the night, and she knew that Cody felt it too.

They were the prodigal children, home again at last, squarely facing the mountains that were the symbols of their past, letting them bear witness to the beginning of their future. There was a strange comfort in knowing that the mountains remained unchanged; that they looked down on Tana and Cody just as they had looked down on their parents, and their grandparents, and all those who had gone before.

'My dad used to say that land never really belonged to

anybody,' Cody murmured. 'That it was the people who belonged to the land.'

Tana stepped closer into the circle of his arm and slipped both hands under his parka and around his waist, a little bemused because the gesture was so comfortable, so familiar. It seemed more suited to a couple who had been together for years than to one looking to the years ahead.

'My folks used to walk out here at night,' she mused, remembering how small her parents had looked from her bedroom window, how earnestly her young mind had pondered the peculiarities of adults who would choose to walk together in the biting cold of a winter night.

'Mine, too.'

She smiled to hear the steady, comforting beat of his heart beneath her ear. 'I feel like just another act in a long-running play. The characters keep changing, and only the backdrop remains the same. I wonder if the mountains get tired of seeing the same old story, generation after generation.'

'I don't think so,' he murmured, turning to face her, very deliberately peeling the gloves from his hands and letting them fall to the snow.

His palms were rough on her cheeks, but warm, and she felt the tingle of blood rising to meet them.

As he unzipped his parka, and then hers, spreading it wide to admit his hands, it never occurred to her to mention the bitter cold, the frosty plumes of their breath that collided and shattered between them; and as they both dropped to their knees in the snow, their bodies pressed so tightly together that not even the moonlight could find space between them, it never occurred to her to be embarrassed by the presence of quiet witnesses. This was the way it should be, kneeling on the altar of their past and their future, offering up the only sacrifice that was appropriate, and somehow it seemed right that the mountains should watch.

PASSPORT TO ROMANCE VACATION SWEEPSTAKES

OFFICIAL RULES

SWEEPSTAKES RULES AND REGULATIONS. NO PURCHASE NECESSARY.

HOW TO ENTER:

1. To enter, complete this official entry form and return with your invoice in the envelope provided, or print your name, address, telephone number and age on a plain piece of paper and mail to: Passport to Romance, P.O. Box #1397, Buffalo, N.Y. 14269-1397. No mechanically reproduced entries accepted.

2. All entries must be received by the Contest Closing Date, midnight, December 31, 1990 to be eligible.

3. Prizes: There will be ten (10) Grand Prizes awarded, each consisting of a choice of a trip for two people to: i) London, England (approximate retail value $5,050 U.S.); ii) England, Wales and Scotland (approximate retail value $6,400 U.S.); iii) Caribbean Cruise (approximate retail value $7,300 U.S.); iv) Hawaii (approximate retail value $ 9,550 U.S.); v) Greek Island Cruise in the Mediterranean (approximate retail value $12,250 U.S.); vi) France (approximate retail value $7,300 U.S.).

4. Any winner may choose to receive any trip or a cash alternative prize of $5,000.00 U.S. in lieu of the trip.

5. Odds of winning depend on number of entries received.

6. A random draw will be made by Nielsen Promotion Services, an independent judging organization on January 29, 1991, in Buffalo, N.Y., at 11:30 a.m. from all eligible entries received on or before the Contest Closing Date. Any Canadian entrants who are selected must correctly answer a time-limited, mathematical skill-testing question in order to win. Quebec residents may submit any litigation respecting the conduct and awarding of a prize in this contest to the Régie des loteries et courses du Quebec.

7. Full contest rules may be obtained by sending a stamped, self-addressed envelope to: "Passport to Romance Rules Request", P.O. Box 9998, Saint John, New Brunswick, E2L 4N4.

8. Payment of taxes other than air and hotel taxes is the sole responsibility of the winner.

9. Void where prohibited by law.

PASSPORT TO ROMANCE VACATION SWEEPSTAKES

OFFICIAL RULES

SWEEPSTAKES RULES AND REGULATIONS. NO PURCHASE NECESSARY.

HOW TO ENTER:

1. To enter, complete this official entry form and return with your invoice in the envelope provided, or print your name, address, telephone number and age on a plain piece of paper and mail to: Passport to Romance, P.O. Box #1397, Buffalo, N.Y. 14269-1397. No mechanically reproduced entries accepted.

2. All entries must be received by the Contest Closing Date, midnight, December 31, 1990 to be eligible.

3. Prizes: There will be ten (10) Grand Prizes awarded, each consisting of a choice of a trip for two people to: i) London, England (approximate retail value $5,050 U.S.); ii) England, Wales and Scotland (approximate retail value $6,400 U.S.); iii) Caribbean Cruise (approximate retail value $7,300 U.S.); iv) Hawaii (approximate retail value $ 9,550 U.S.); v) Greek Island Cruise in the Mediterranean (approximate retail value $12,250 U.S.); vi) France (approximate retail value $7,300 U.S.).

4. Any winner may choose to receive any trip or a cash alternative prize of $5,000.00 U.S. in lieu of the trip.

5. Odds of winning depend on number of entries received.

6. A random draw will be made by Nielsen Promotion Services, an independent judging organization on January 29, 1991, in Buffalo, N.Y., at 11:30 a.m. from all eligible entries received on or before the Contest Closing Date. Any Canadian entrants who are selected must correctly answer a time-limited, mathematical skill-testing question in order to win. Quebec residents may submit any litigation respecting the conduct and awarding of a prize in this contest to the Régie des loteries et courses du Quebec.

7. Full contest rules may be obtained by sending a stamped, self-addressed envelope to: "Passport to Romance Rules Request", P.O. Box 9998, Saint John, New Brunswick, E2L 4N4.

8. Payment of taxes other than air and hotel taxes is the sole responsibility of the winner

9. Void where prohibited by law.